A Different
BALL GAME

A Different
BALL GAME

BOB THOMSON

Library of Congress Control Number: 2012905325

ISBN:	Hardcover	978-1-4691-8811-9
	Softcover	978-1-4691-8810-2
	Ebook	978-1-4691-8812-6

This book was printed in the United States of America.

To order additional copies of this book, contact:
Xlibris Corporation
1-888-795-4274
www.Xlibris.com
Orders@Xlibris.com
114048

PRELUDE

THIS IS A STORY ABOUT a one-armed man that lost his left arm because of a motorcycle accident and has had a hard time trying to adjust and live a normal as can be life and learning to cope with everyday problems.

In 1974 there was a period in the U. S. A. which it was hard to get gasoline at the pumps because there was a gasoline shortage. (There were lines at the pumps.) People would wait for their turn to get gas at service stations across the country when a station got gas. Many purchased motorcycles to get around on using a lot less gas.

The man in this story was in a crash, when a car pulled out in front of him and got T-boned by his motorcycle, resulting in a spinal nerve injury which caused the loss and eventual dismembering of his left arm, by choice, because of no motor nerves to use this arm which was now useless. This accident was so severe that neither vehicle could be repaired, and he was left in a coma for a month.

He married under the heavy medication, soon after and that marriage didn't work out without love, a few years later, he married again and after only six months found her in a motel with a 16-year-old boy and that was the end of that marriage. He is now 45 years old and the first wife and their two girls were in Pennsylvania after a divorce in 1973, and he was 26 years old at the time of divorce. The time of the accident was in October of 1974.

The next two years was spent running around to different V. A. hospitals try to cope with the severe phantom limb pain resulting from the spinal nerve injury that was causing the left hand and arm to feel as if it was crushed and was causing severe un-ending pain 24 hours a day.

The Red Cross got this man on non-service connected disability because of his Army obligation was fulfilled. He was told he couldn't get Social Security disability because of his two years of college at Penn State University.

After receiving a small settlement from the accident he purchased a home and thought he was destined to be a loner and just about gave up on getting another wife until his father gave him another place in East Texas at Pine Lake Reservoir and that is where this story begins.

After looking at all of his triumphs and tribulations makes you wonder if Hell isn't living on earth . . . for some of us.

My Dad was pretty well off because he had retired as an insurance agent and worked till he was 70. He explained to me his retirement was a lot more that way. Anyway it enabled him to enjoy a wife and a girlfriend at the same time, and be able to furnish two women with a place to live and have kids from both. You see when my Mom was married to him and he was in the Air Force in Alexandria, LA. He was stationed in that city. You see back then he had a girlfriend in Alexandria and only came home on leave to visit his wife (my Mom) and family—my brother and I.

Now years later the girlfriend at that time turned into his wife and he divorced my Mom. And now again years later he has divorced this one and now married the next in line and he had three boys and three girls from the second wife. Now he only has one son from the third girlfriend-wife. He had bought a lot in Pine Lake Reservoir for his latest wife so they could live there after retirement. This is the lot he would later give to me.

MY STORY DEC. 2, 09

IN 1987 I WENT TO visit my Dad in Alexandria, Louisiana and enjoyed crappie fishing with him and met his girlfriend that had had a stepbrother for me to meet. Well he was letting this lady live in one of his rent houses free because she was the mother of my stepbrother. My Dad now owned the lot in a subdivision at Pine Lake. We went over there several times and cleared off the lot and he then ask me if I would like to live there beside him. He would buy the lot next door. After returning home to Owl Creek Park in Bell County, Texas, not far from Temple, Texas, I thought about it for a few months and decided maybe I would have a better life at the larger lake and decided I would give it a try. I started trot line fishing and it was hard because I had lost my left arm in a motorcycle accident in my home town of Gatesville, Texas back in 1974. I was on V. A. disability but it was non-service connected. Now my Dad and his wife got a divorce because of the fights about the lady with his son born in 1974.

Now after buying the lot next door and moving a trailer in on his lot, him and his girlfriend decide she doesn't want to live at the lake and he ends up giving me both lots and the trailer because now they are going to build them a new home at Cotile Lake just north of Alexandria. After a few months I was doing quite well selling catfish and stayed pretty busy just fishing. I also enjoyed playing golf. I took a set of golf clubs and cut them off about six inches and fabricated fiberglass grips on them that helped me with direction.

In the summer of 1989 I had drank some lake water one day right out of the lake, I was so hot and thirsty. A couple of days later found myself at the dentist office in Hilltown, Texas with a severe tooth ache. As I pulled into the dentist office driveway a 1966 Ford two door hardtop pulled in behind me and the motor revved up and the gal driving was letting her presence be known by sounding off her dual straight pipe exhaust system. It really sounded nice to me. She had no idea I was a hot-rod person.

As we sat in the waiting room waiting to be called this gal's mother kept eyeing me and smiling as I was reading a book. Occasionally I would look up and her and her daughter would whisper to each other and smile at me. The mother looked to be about 70 and the daughter looked to be about 20 to 22 years old. After waiting so long and finally when the daughter's eyes and mine stopped on each other I said, "I like your car." She said thank you and ask me if I would like to go out and look at it closer. I looked it over and told her about some of my latest rods, one of which was a 1931 Model A sedan and the other a 1930 Chevy roadster. We hit it off real well and I told her I had just moved to town and she ask me if I would call her sometime and already had her phone number and name written on a piece of paper and handed it to me. I told her I fished a lot and she said she likes to fish.

I felt so bad as I was 46 years old and just knew if she knew that I wouldn't be of interest anymore so I thought. Anyway about 3 months later I was still bored and was always thinking of calling her but kept thinking I was too old for her. So one day I called her up and she was staying with her mother in low-income housing in Hilltown. She said she wondered if I was ever going to call her, yes, come on over.

So I went over and all the way was scared of what to say. We visited for about an hour outside in the parking lot and she was looking at my truck and had to ask me why I had a bottom half of a white styrofoam cup on the passenger door. I had to explain that where I deer hunted the deer where so close to where I parked the truck, I was driving along and loading my lever action 30-30 while driving and it was so early it was still dark and when I closed the lever while the rifle was laying on the seat pointing away from me the seat belt buckle was under the gun and put pressure on the trigger as I closed the lever causing the gun to go off, scaring me big time. The bullet went through the passenger door and left an inverted funnel-type hole. I super-glued a cup over the hole to hide it until I could fix it. It was embarrassing but at the same time pretty funny. It gave us a good laugh and we began hitting it right off.

As I was leaving she ask me how old I was and I said, "Gee, I knew you were going to ask me that," and I said "That is why I haven't called before now because I didn't know how I was going to explain why I even called because I am so much older than you." She said, "Let me be the judge of that." I said "46, I'm way too old for you—how old are you?" She said "24." She then said, "Will you take me fishing sometime?" Later I found out all the guys she had dated were duds and that her mom wanted her to see what I was like for her daughter.

We had such a good time fishing and enjoyed each other's company so much we were together a lot now and we learned more about each other. I found out that she had just got back from being in the Coast Guard and had failed to be able to swim the distance required of all Coast Guard graduates. She had passed everything else and excelled in marksmanship with a rifle.

After about a month we were now kissing, cuddling and acting like teenagers. I had never dated a girl with such a small thin frame that had such large boobs. Her mom steadily called to check on her and she was always expected to be back by dark. One time coming back from going to Walmart, we had headed home in time but my universal joint on the drive shaft of the truck started vibrating and squealing so bad I had to go real slow and that put us at my house after dark and her mom had a fit. She told her mom that she might have to stay the night because I couldn't drive my truck and her car was at her mom's and her mom didn't drive. Well, her mom got an aunt to come get her. I thought that was kind of amusing. Here I am nearly half a century old and mom worried about her daughter that had been in the Coast Guard and now back at home. I took it as love for her only daughter.

A few months went by and the petting got heavier but I was still not allowed to go all the way but there wasn't any talk of marriage yet. Now that she knows of me doing paint and body work we took all the chrome off of her 66 Fairlane 500 and I gave it a pretty coat of red flames and put the nose in burnt orange that went into orange into yellow flames and put large racing numbers 66 on the doors. That tickled her to death.

We camped in my truck one night as it was now May of 1989 and in the last few months mom had gotten used to her coming and going as she pleased. We made love for the first time in my Jimmy Hoffa truck I called it as we had just learned the missing Jimmy Hoffa was put in a car crusher in 1976. That was the year of my Chevy truck. I figured there might be some of his body fluids in my truck. Now a lot had been going on behind the scenes while Barb and I were dating so heavy. My mom and stepfather had come over and purchased two house trailers and three lots just up the street from where my trailer was located and come over to surprise me with their purchase and I was a little displeased because I told them the reason my real dad had given this property to me that the subdivision was a terrible place and that they would have to pay dues on those three lots. They disagreed and said nobody told them anything about dues.

Also Barb's mom had gotten back together with her ex-husband as she was a mail-order bride from California. That's why Barb was born in California and now in Hilltown, Texas. That was the real reason the pressure was off of us and I didn't know that. He was a lot older than Barb's mom.

Mom and my stepfather finally got a huge bill from previous owners' back dues and it made my stepfather so mad he paid up all the dues and gave both house trailers and the three lots to me. Barb must think my families are rich since I have just been given one trailer with two lots from my real dad and two home trailers and three lots from my mom and stepfather.

The deal was, back in 1974, developers bought up some acreage and turned it into a high-class setup on Pine Lake land to be run by a board of directors and have a golf course, restaurant and swimming pool. Over a few years the developers sold enough lots at $1800 apiece for the house, 30' by 80' trailer lots and no telling how much for the 200' by 300' lots for houses. Anyway, the dues were only $5.00 per lot. It didn't matter what they were. The developers were to come back in after most of the lots were sold and pave the streets, because now they only had a thin asphalt coating that was full of holes. Actually, I found out later that there were really two different subdivisions that had been joined together and that the county road that now separates the house side of the subdivision from the trailer house side was really one of the subdivision's streets, and was given to the county by the subdivision.

A few weeks later, Barb had been getting sick in the morning, and her mom told her she was pregnant. Barb kept telling her we hadn't done anything to get her that way, but she did get a doctor's appointment, and they did do a pregnancy test. It was positive. I asked her if she wanted to marry me, and she didn't know just yet, because she still couldn't believe she was pregnant. I remember she would tell about when the doctor told her she was pregnant. The doctor was probably 70 years old, and she said "Well, how did that happen?" and he about went to his knees laughing, and said "Well, how do you THINK it happened?"

We decided to get married on July 4, 1989. We went to the courthouse, and one of her stepfather's friends who was a J. P. married us. Now that we were married, we had to re-evaluate everything. I was living on a mere $500 a month non-service-connected VA pension for disability. I found a buy on a couple bundles of raw lumber and bought an old homemade round-bale hay trailer made out of old drillstem pipe tubing to haul the lumber home.

When I was measuring off the floor plan for the building, a young black man was walking down the county road that bordered our place. He said "Hi, you doin' all right?" and I said "Yeah, fine," and he could see I was getting into a big job for a one-armed guy. He didn't get far by me when I said "Are you broke down?" and he said "Yeah, starter went out in my old truck." I said, "How far you gotta go to get one?" and he said "All the way to Hilltown," which was about 15 miles. I said "The keys are in that blue truck sitting there, if you want to use it." He was all white teeth, smiling so big. He said "You sure?" and I said "Yeah, go ahead." He walked back to me, shook my hand and said "I sure would appreciate it." He couldn't believe it, but jumped on it, and came back by a short time later and said "He'll put the starter in and bring my truck right back." His name was Willie Hington, and everyone called him Poochie.

After bringing my truck back, he asked me if I needed any help, and I said it would be nice but I didn't have any money to spend on wages. He said he was out of work and would help for nothing for a while. I said "Sounds good to me," so we framed out a 20-foot by 30-foot garage with a 10-foot ceiling. Most of my lumber was ruff cut to 2" x 4" and 2" x 11"—I mean a full 2" width by a full 4". He said he had done some body and paint work before and could get us some jobs, so we were off and rolling. We covered the building in plastic for the first few jobs until we had some money for siding and plywood for the top. I wasn't allowed to have a business in the subdivision, so we did it for friends, but charged them.

As time went on, Barb's tummy kept getting bigger and bigger, and I had agreed to a vasectomy so we wouldn't have to worry about more kids. I started playing more golf and fishing a lot less, even though we got a dock boat with a lot bigger motor on it. I was really enjoying the golf tournaments until someone protested me because I dragged the stick of an electric welder across the face of my irons and it left little bumps, which made my balls do a backspin on the green. They gave me such a hard time that I quit playing. My wife was also nagging at me when I spent too much time on the course. They tried to get me to come back and play, but I said no, I just played for fun, and I didn't want all the arguments. They eventually said that since I only had one arm, they didn't care what I did to those clubs, but I said "No, I see your true colors." You know, the bad part about quitting was that since the subdivision hadn't taken care of the golf course in years, a few of my friends and I dug in the pipes for watering the golf course and their dads contributed the money to buy the PVC pipe and rent the ditch witch to make it all possible. We even dug a huge hole and put in a pond to hold water to irrigate with. A retired serviceman was able to borrow a small bulldozer for the pond excavating.

One day, while Poochie and I were duck hunting at the lake behind the house, we kept hearing a car horn and loud exhaust pipes racking off. I said to Poochie, "We better go—I know my wife is not due for another month but that sure sounds like her Ford." Her water had broken and she couldn't find me! We had been going to a doctor in Kenter, Texas once a month on a pay-as-you-go baby program, and the doctor had told us just a week before that it would be a while yet before she had the baby. I rushed home and it was her, all right, and I had to listen to her yakking at me—where was I when she needed me? If she would have honked the horn while sitting in the driveway, I would have known sooner that it was her, because the lake was only four hundred yards from us. We both had everything ready to go, as it was 60 miles to Kenter, and it was all good road.

She stayed in the labor room for a few hours, and the way she was wailing, it must have been some really bad pain she was having. I got hungry and went to get a hamburger. She wasn't supposed to eat anything, but she talked me out of over half of it. In a few more hours, the baby started coming on and the lady doctor had gone on home. The two remaining ladies had delivered most of Dr. Alandator's babies, so they were well experienced. I stood there and watched my own baby being born, and it was a shocking experience, especially when they had to spank her hard several times before she cried. I was in tears for both mama and baby, and you could hear mama scream out in the parking lot, I'm sure. After the baby was born, we gave her a name—June Julee Roberts.

In the rush, Barb had left one of the packed bags at home, so I had to go get it. It began raining and freezing on the way, so I spent the night at home so I could better drive on ice in daylight on the way back. It was December 21, 1990. Everything went fine, so she didn't have to stay another night, and we could leave and get home before the roads turned into ice at night again. We had a lot of friends wanting to come in the house to see our baby, but my wife kept her away from everyone for about a week because she was afraid of germs in the winter months. I didn't get to hold our baby because I had only one arm, and might drop her.

For Christmas I got my wife a new Yamaha four-wheeler, and she really liked that, being a deprived youngster herself. My wife had told me tales of how she went without eating and had rags for clothes, and the Greyhound buses, and different men her mom tried to marry. I guess Barb's mom was Blackfoot Indian and had had a hard life.

Her mom invited us out to their place on Rosy Ridge one weekend, and we went to show the baby and meet her folks properly. I understood why she hadn't wanted me to meet them after we got there. Everybody called this 81-year-old guy "Pop." He had taken on Barb's mom to be his wife, then kicked her out, and now taken her back. The house we went into was a small one-room shack built out of 1x8 pine boards. The knotholes had fallen out of some boards, and they had shrunk so much you could look between them and see outside. There wasn't even an outhouse—you had to go outside behind a tree or bush. Pop was out there when we got there—he was down at the creek checking on the cows. When he drove up, he was a delightful old man, continuously laughing at everything. He shook my hand vigorously, and said "Hey, why don't you and I go to town and get us all a hamburger?" I said, "Sounds like a plan to me!"

His two boys had nice brick homes, and one lived on the same property. I asked him whose home was there, and pointed. He said "One of my boys." We had to turn around and go back because steam was coming out from under the hood of the '68 Ford ¾ ton truck, which was rusty with no paint left on the body. He said "We'd better let her cool off a minute, and I'll re-wrap that top hose with some new duct tape I just bought the other day." I watched him wrap the top radiator hose and stretch the duct tape tight to squeeze down into the V's of the hose, as it was not a pre-shaped hose but one of those with all the ribs so you can bend them without collapsing. I couldn't believe he could think that would get us to town and back, even though town was only about 5 minutes away. He was 81 years old, a short, skinny man who had surveyed for a living.

After going 70 mph for about 3 miles on the highway, he grabbed the steering wheel with both hands and slammed on the brakes. He left skid marks for about 60 feet and then down-shifted, as it was a floor shift with a granny gear. I had straight-armed the dash to keep off of it. He slid right up in the grass next to the 60-foot-tall pine trees and jumped out, saying "Gotta take a dump." Pretty embarrassing to have to wait in the truck with traffic passing in both directions and him behind a single pine with no brush around. I couldn't see him, but traffic coming both ways could see him squatting bare-assed.

I looked at the tree and saw an arm reaching out, and a hand raking up pine straw, so I just slunk down in the seat like I was a little tiny person. He got back in, slammed the door and said "Sorry for the delay." I said "Oh, that's OK, when you gotta go, you gotta go." We went to the Dairy Queen and got four burgers, fries and drinks. We headed home with no steam from under the hood . . . yet. When we got back, he put the bags up on the table and grabbed one to open for me because I only had one arm. I grabbed one and said, "No, I don't need any help. Watch this." I had to be super fast because I knew his fingers had to get through those pine needles, and I could open my own hamburger.

Upon leaving, my wife apologized for the conditions there, and I said "That's no reflection on you. You keep our place clean and that's all I care about. She washed and waxed her car every 3 or 4 days, too. This was the place Barb grew up in as a youngster, and she was ashamed of it. That was the only time we ever went out to the farm.

About a year after this, Pop died, and left a little '76 Ford Ranger truck to Barb. The motor was worn out. It was a 4-cylinder.

June was only about two years old when our problems started with Pine Harbor Property Owners' Association. I had rented out the trailer house my dad had given me, and it was hard to collect rent. I had to re-rent it several times and keep paying the taxes and dues, so I decided to sell it. So we sold it to one of those self-ordained-preacher type of guys, but he also had a job in Temple-Inland Sawmill in Pineville, Texas. It was with a down payment and monthly payments, rent-to-own. Another big mistake. Had to kick him out too and still pay dues and taxes, and he was the filthiest of them all. June spent a lot of time strapped in a child's car seat bolted to the front rack of that Yamaha 2-wheel-drive four-wheeler, as Barb rode it every day all over the back country roads.

The subdivision kept hounding us for dues all the time, and there was a lady that bought a big restaurant down at the highway called Chateau Shores and it also had cabins and house trailers for rent, and also bought a house in the subdivision. Their last name was Gore and they had moved here from the Philippines where he had a radiator shop. They changed the name of the restaurant to Gore's and when it never got going, they sold the pine trees off to make their payments on the place. They also bought a home in the subdivision. She got on the property owners' association and then got her real estate license and called her business Lake Properties.

Now in the fall of 1994, we put our 4-year-old daughter on a school bus for the first time as now kids had to go to what they call pre-kindergarten. I got the trailer house and two lots back as the preacher got so far behind on the taxes and dues so we sold it real cheap to some people far enough away they hadn't heard of all the people's problems in our subdivision. They wanted to pay the dues and taxes themselves and I knocked them off the price I got for the place. It was worth it to get it out of my name. I had no idea that letting them pay taxes and dues would get me a summary judgment in my lawsuit later.

The association spent their dues on the house side of the subdivision and called us trailer trash in their little board meetings. Their streets were in good shape, and ours were potholes. Ron Cole came down from Oklahoma, where he lived, for retirement after the Oklahoma City bombing and bought a house near the lake and made friends with us, as we used to take our little one June to the park by their house. He even baby-sat for us while my wife and I went fishing in the boat, as the boat ramp was by their house. They made good friends, we thought. Everyone in the subdivision always stayed stirred up and unhappy because the place was so crooked as far as all the money went to the house side. We even paid up our delinquent dues when we sold the trailer, hoping they would do some improvements on our side.

I made a good friend on the golf course named Andy Andrews, and we even went hunting together. They also baby-sat for us sometimes, and were good friends. At times we even went to their house on the house side and ate barbecue with them. We even made friends out in the boat fishing. One new friend even lived in the subdivision, named Clarence Grady. I painted his Mercury boat motor for him, as it was corroded from different times he had taken it to the coast. Salt water is hard on aluminum. It ended up I started going over to Clarence's a lot, because after Mrs. Gore got on the board and became president of the subdivision, they were going to start suing people and foreclosing on people who wouldn't pay dues.

Now here I was, on non-service-connected VA disability, about $600 a month in 1995, and the cost of living was increasing a lot as compared to a couple years ago. At this time my wife and I got mad at the subdivision, and we started writing letters in the local newspaper. "Double for Nothing" was the title, because we owned 3 little lots and were being charged 21 dollars a month for our place which measured 82 feet by 90 feet, while the people on the board almost entirely of people from the house side were only paying 7 dollars a month for a piece of property 200 x 250 feet. This made a lot of enemies. To get people on the trailer side to pay dues, the board decided to improve our streets. They got a small-time paving company to repair about a half mile of street on the trailer side, as the trailer side only had one street coming off the main road. The paving job consisted of driving an oil truck down the road and another truck dropping a thin layer of gravel onto the oil. It was a mess. The oil got on everyone's cars and trucks, it shifted into piles and worse, ended up in the culverts blocking the rain runoff. The paving job ended up being a joke.

We now were presented with a new problem. Every time there was a new election of board members, they would find new ways to threaten people to pay their dues. Now we had some big high rollers move into the subdivision that were going to change things. They turned over the properties that hadn't paid their dues for years to the school department for foreclosures. Since we were not paying our dues on purpose because of all the corruption in the management of the subdivision, we feared they might try to do that with us. They started to send us letters of foreclosure to threaten us, but the more I talked to Clarence Grady, the less I feared foreclosure because of all the dirt I had dug up on the subdivision.

My wife and I lost lots of sleep worrying about all our problems with the subdivision and our daughter was now getting old enough to feel all the pressure. Clarence told me that when he was president of the subdivision, that a few of the elite board members—one I'll never forget was by the name of Cheatroe, which I thought was very fitting—him and a few others that were wealthy or at least appeared to be. The mom and dad of my two young friends were on the board of directors of the property owners' association of the subdivision. These two young boys and the dad were the ones that revived the golf course that had been forgotten for years. Well, when Mrs. Boden opposed a lot of things the new board did that was against the laws & bylaws of the subdivision, she was kicked off the board because of the new guys that took over the subdivision by developing a clique to run is as they wanted to be run, with no regard for the laws and bylaws that were to keep it from being run by a few. Mrs. Boden wasn't really kicked off the board, though—at election time once a year, the election committee was part of the good old boys and told her she didn't even get one vote and laughed in her face. We had already lost the yacht club, which had a restaurant and boat ramps, to a man named Bob Billings, who bought it somehow without the people voting on it, and we had already lost the swimming pool and its facilities. Clarence Grady, the man who used to be the president of Pine Harbor Property Owners' Association, was filling me in on all the violations for years. He told me how Mr. Cheatroe had used the money allotted for street repairs and taken his wife and a couple other cronies on a cruise. You see, the developers had only put down temporary streets so they could sell lots of the acres they had purchased.

I had made friends by now with a few of the black population behind the subdivision, and one day while laying out a foundation for an addition I was going to build onto my trailer house, one of these new black friends told me of how his people had lost the land to the developers. Back in 1964, some wheeler-dealers found out the Saline River was going to be dammed and the only bridge across it was going to be at this spot, which was going to make the land value jump 100 times what it had been. Well, these men in suits and ties contacted the land owners which were all black, and told them they would trade them twice as much land and pay them too. It seemed like a good deal, but after talking it over, they refused. The men came back and kept making them better offers because these man knew where the boundaries of the proposed lake would be, and this land would soon become lakefront property after the lake was filled up. The name of the new man-made lake was to be called Pine Lake. This lake would separate Louisiana and Texas by a 70-mile-long lake and be 2 to 3 miles wide.

Well, these men devised a new plan and came back one more time and told the black people "Sorry, we can't do business, but we need to inform you that they were going to put in an airport just north of your properties and you may be too unhappy here because of the airplanes landing and taking off over your houses at all hours of the day." The black people talked this over and came back to the wheeler-dealers for negotiations. They finally agreed to settle for some acreage back farther away from the lake, and they are still there today.

The subdivision was finally opened in 1974, and the lake was completed. It was supposed to take 2 years to fill up, but an unusual amount of rainfall in 1966 filled it up in only 6 months. It was comparable to a gold rush—people from all over, especially retiring people wanting a place to enjoy their last days on this planet in a beautiful climate and environment, flocked to the newly developed Bass Capital of the World, as they called it. The lake was stocked with tons of fingerling bass. The lake was also stocked with a bass called Striper, which grew well, and it didn't take long for the lake to become the Bass Capital of the World as the warm waters and abundance of shade let these fish grow to enormous size. This led many retired people to become fishing guides, and with all the advertisement of the lake and success of catching lots of fish made the lake a haven for weekend fishermen from all over the country.

After learning some history of the lake and the subdivision, I realized now why the subdivision was in such turmoil. These older folks that had bought into the subdivision were retirement age when they purchased their lots and built their homes. Now by the time I moved here, the houses and lots weren't worth but a fraction of what was spent on them because of lost interest in them, people that have aged and a number of people that have died of old age. Then I found out that there were two subdivisions that were put together, and the bylaws used to read that people that didn't use the golf course or the yacht club did not have to pay dues. All this knowledge was good for me to know in case I ever got sued for non-payment of dues.

In the meantime, I was continuing to build on to a house trailer and ended up making it two large rooms on a concrete slab. Willie Hington (my black friend) helped me pour and finish the concrete slab. The rooms were about 17 feet x 18 feet, one on top of the other. To get the money for this, I had sold one house trailer and bought and sold a few boats and trucks I had repaired and painted. My VA disability was also raised because of getting married and having a child.

Now all this time, my daughter had started school, and I remember both of us crying as she got on a school bus for the first time as she was now only five years old and was one of the first to start at that age because now they had started what they called Pre-K or pre-kindergarten. Gosh, she was so tiny to go off without a parent.

About this time is when my mom and stepfather decided they were missing out on not being around their new grandbaby and decided to sell out in Gatesville, Texas, 250 miles away, and bought a place in town 12 miles away so they could be around to watch and enjoy their grandbaby (June) grow up.

My wife and I were truly enjoying an easy life and we got to where we went fishing almost every day. We went in the morning and in the evening as the fish would tear up the surface of the water like piranhas on a feeding frenzy. We used baby-sitters a lot and really had a ball catching bass and stripers as fast as we could get them unhooked and re-cast. We hardly ever brought any home to cook. We just enjoyed the hard fighting fish and released them back.

One day when I thought we were on top of the world with building a better house and more business body work and painting, we had a man from downtown deliver our papers that we were being sued by the subdivision. My wife went through the roof and I told her not to worry, that we paid our taxes and that we were homesteaded with a child in school and they couldn't take our home away from us. That didn't seem to help calm her down any.

The judge was a good friend of my wife's and I went and had a talk with him on this matter. I had talked to him before, and he told me first to pay a little each month, and we would be okay. I didn't want this and I got a petition up and I got about 90% of the people living there to sign it as we no longer wished to be a part of the subdivision. This petition was for the house trailer side, and explained how the people were unhappy because the dues went to the house side of the subdivision, and we paid every 30 feet the same amount the house side paid for 200-foot lots. I took the petition to the county attorney and he just laughed at me and refused to do anything. I didn't know that the subdivision had just hired him in his private practice to represent them in a lawsuit against the Bodens. The same man that spent his own money, and his two boys and others had restored the golf course. The same lady they had just kicked off the board of directors.

It seemed as though everything was against us.

We began framing our two rooms about this time, and it was taking my mind off all the problems, but we were losing a lot of sleep over worrying about how to deal with this gigantic new problem. It appeared at first it was not bothering our friends around the subdivision, but they were just being nice to us because of our daughter, who was about six years old now.

Here I was being sued by the subdivision and building a house, framing out the walls and no one offered to help, and I only had one arm, doing it by myself. One of the men I played golf with and hunted with stayed my buddy and he had retired out of the military service. Even though he had lots of friends on the board and lived on the house side. The county road was between the house side and the trailer side, but I had learned that that was one of our former streets of the subdivision that the board members had donated to the county years ago.

After the Bodens were sued, they asked us if we wanted to be a part of their lawsuit and it didn't take a minute to decide yes, we sure would. In the meantime, I counter-sued the subdivision and would represent myself. The subdivision had a hard time trying to find a legal laws and bylaws to suit us by, as their records had been destroyed. Anyway, the war was on. I spent a lot of time at the courthouse, digging up records and false promises of the subdivision for court.

There was a lot of tension at home, and it was affecting our little one a lot. She would cry and ask if we were going to lose our home all the time. It really put a lot of pressure on family life. We still went fishing, still continued on the house, still used our babysitters, and they were calming our daughter a lot. They were always hugging her and buying her presents and such. We didn't have any babysitters on the house trailer side. They were people that were well off and lived in homes in the subdivision. We always thought how nice these people were to us.

As I was building my add-on and making my court appearances, we had some friends that lived down the street that the wife was always coming up to watch me work. We talked subdivision, and what I was going to present at court the next session. Little did I know that she was in cahoots with the board members and I was losing all my surprises for the attorney against me. You see, lawyers hate to come up against someone who represents themselves because lawyers are like brothers and tend to make lawsuits last longer and talk to each other without either party knowing what is going on under them. I would go and have something entered just before court and the opposing attorney would not have a chance to be prepared for that topic. Now they had the wife as a double agent.

Now a new problem. Andy Andrews (my hunting buddy)'s son in law had lost his job, and he was a welder. He was living in Houston, in a tent, and doing odd jobs. Well, Andy talked to his friends on the board, and the lady that had bought the Chateau Shores restaurant that didn't make it was now a realtor and was the new president of the subdivision. They decided they would fence in the subdivision with hogwire fence and they would put up an electronic gate, and that way could get rid of the guards at the guard shack, and it would make Andy's son-in-law a lot of money welding up the new steel gates for the subdivision. All we wanted was for the subdivision to fix our streets that were so full of potholes, but now they started fencing us off like we were prisoners or something.

One day Andy came by and asked me if I had any objections to the fence. I said yes, I didn't use the subdivision streets because they were so crooked and windy and full of holes. He told me they couldn't put the fence up on anyone that objected, since fences were illegal in the subdivision. So they put it up along the whole length of the subdivision on the county road, with me being the only exception, which made me look bad again.

Our daughter was beginning to have trouble at school and on the bus. Kids harassing her on the bus, and a couple of school teachers lived on the house side. We were living in hell, it seemed. Our daughter didn't have any friends any longer, and we ended up driving her to and from school every day. About a month later, Nick Serino, Andy's son-in-law, was put in charge over the guards, and he came and paid me a visit. This was about the same time we found out that Andy was ailing and was diagnosed with cancer, and didn't have but about six months to live. Well, Nick wasn't very pleasant. He threatened me while carrying an assault weapon and told me I'd better not resist them putting a fence up on the county road. I immediately called the Justice of the Peace and reported it. He was the same man that married my wife and me. He said he would make a mental note of it. What a letdown, I thought. Are the cards stacked against us or what? The worst part was trying to raise a daughter in all of this mess. The government had just passed a new law called about a violistic threat, and here's a guy with an assault weapon and I can't do anything about it. My wife would cry sometimes until she trembled.

Our lawsuit was now about a year old, and the district judge kept siding with me and trying to get the subdivision to change some of their ways. The attorney against me was given a lifetime membership on our private golf course and a free lot. The sign on hole #1 had been taken down, as it read "Only property owners or house guests are allowed on the course."

June kept getting seasick on the bus, and we talked to the bus driver, which was a young lady that knew my wife in school. My wife couldn't believe she could get a job as a school bus driver because the gal was such a party lady and liked her fast life. Even at that, they got along, and would even wait for the bus and go out and sometimes visit with her, because it was at the end of the bus run, and my wife and her could talk a couple of minutes as there would only be a couple kids on the bus left to drop off. That made it easier to talk to, and this lady would help us with the problem. Some of the young black girls wore loud smelling perfume that would trigger June's stomach and she would be motion sick. Anyway, this bus driver tried pulling June up front on the bus, tried it with her sitting by an open window and everything, but she still would throw up and sometimes get it on her own clothes. We couldn't afford to drive June back and forth, so we really tried to keep her on the bus somehow. My wife had been telling me that she thought this gal was drinking mixed drinks in a paper cup when she dropped June off, because when she would talk to her as June was getting off of the bus, she could smell whiskey. I said "Are you sure?" and Barb would say, "It sure smells like it." She didn't appear to be drunk, but it still bothered my wife.

One day a man was driving the bus and dropped June off, and her mom asked June where was Diane, and June said "Well, I think she's in jail." June told a wild tale about how she was asleep in the morning and in the seat of the bus on the way to school, and she woke up on the floor of the bus with an older kid on top of her. June said a couple deer ran out in front of the school bus, and Diane dodged them, because the bus went off the road and into the woods and was bouncing the kids all over and everyone was screaming and one kid pushed June on the floor and got over her to protect her, as to save her from harm, and when they got to town she side-swiped a pickup truck and the pickup truck followed the bus to school to collect for damages. My wife called around and found out this was true, and even read in the newspaper that the bus driver was given a blood test and was on drugs too. That was June's last ride on a school bus, and the next time my wife saw Diane, she was a janitor at the school and she was dating a schoolteacher.

Now they had leased out our private golf course.

When they put up the fence in my yard and cut me off of about 12 feet of my property on the county road, I tore it down and sold it. They did this about four or five times, and I continued to tear it down as they were just doing it to shake us up and my wife told them, "If you bring another roll of hogwire fence, my husband is going to stick it in your ass crossways." Well, that brought out the sheriff, the judge, the commissioner and a deputy. They were there to put up the fence once and for all. My wife just happened to be parked along the side of the county road, and they told her if she didn't let them put up the fence, she would be put in jail for a violistic threat. She told the sheriff, "You know that big roll of hogwire won't fit in their ass. Why didn't you do anything to Nick Serino when he threatened us with an assault weapon?" We stood by as they put up the fence, and the sheriff kept telling my wife, "You better get in your car before they string the fence, or you will have to walk all the way down to the guard shack and back up the county road to get your car." That was about 1 ½ mile walk to get back to the car. She did not respond to that and kept ignoring him. I had already established in court that hogwire was illegal for use around schools, day care centers or anywhere children were to be kept in. Now here is the law enforcing a wrong doing, unbelievable!

When the fence was done, they laughed at my wife and said, "Enjoy your walk." She now said "Watch this." She walked over to the fence, pushed it down and stepped over, got in her 1981 full-sized Mercury Marquis, and cut the wheels and floorboarded it, and it spun around, and the back tires covered all of us with gravel that stung and the sheriff, judge and commissioner covered their faces and squatted down as they turned their back on the shower of rocks. After they left, I tore the fence down once more. Matter of fact, if they had looked in their rear view mirrors, they could have seen me begin.

Not long after this, we had a storm, and it knocked down lots of trees and tree branches, and as it was in this stacked deck the Bodens had a tree break and fall on their house, and it was huge, and the weight of it went through the roof and it ended up on the floor of their dining room. The Bodens called the tree trimmers to come and remove it and a couple of the board members stopped as the tree trimmers got there and told them they would be arrested if they didn't get out of the subdivision and it was private property and they needed a permit to cut it. This permit thing was something new, and they were punishing the Bodens with it. No wonder the Bodens won their lawsuit a few years later. We eventually dropped out of the Bodens' lawsuit because we were being punished double being in two lawsuits at the same time.

I found a way to keep the fence off of me because I went to the post office and had a mailbox put up at my house, and they had to accept the access to the mailbox because others had mailboxes and openings, but they didn't want us to have one. The three stooges on the board came by one more time to talk to me about the fence, but I ignored them and my wife came out on the porch and started asking, "What do they want?" I said, "Honey, get back in the house, they'll try to get you arrested again. Besides that, they can't even wipe their asses without smearing the shit," and laughed.

After we got the big flat-bottomed boat, we were at the long bridge swimming in the heat of the summer, and I remember thinking about all the different boats we have had at this same spot because the water was shallow and it was easy to get in and out of the boat and the bottom of the lake was smooth and no stumps to trip on. Here my wife didn't make it in the Coast Guard because she couldn't learn how to swim, but it didn't take her long to learn now that she was relaxed and in shoulder-deep water a lot, and the water was warm. Sometimes the water was even hot, and we would swim out to deeper water where we would laugh because the temperature of the water would have cold spots you had to swim through to get back in warmer water. Mom and June used to have to wear swimming aids to keep them afloat, but now they were both swimming and laughing, and enjoyed our outings. We always had our fishing tackle as the fish would tear up the surface about a half hour before dark, and then is when we really had a ball.

We heard that our doctor, Dr. Hocky, had bought a house in the subdivision on the house side over by the boat ramp. That had surprised us, as he owned a beautiful farm out by Pineville, Texas, and it even had a large pond in it which was full of fish. It wasn't long after he bought his house, we read in the newspaper he had been arrested for drugs. I guess he was investigated for selling too many drugs considered speed and too many for pain, and they had a trial over it and he went to prison for a few years.

The back end of the subdivision had a street that led to the county road, and a lot of people used it, but the maintenance men blocked it with a huge mound of dirt and it infuriated a lot of people living near it as our streets were so bad a lot of residents used it as a way out. Well, the neighbors dug it out by hand with shovels, because our streets were so bad. Here the people that paid dues were punished along with the people not paying them.

We were still enjoying our fishing and in the winter I loved the woods and the small mountains reminded me of Pennsylvania where I grew up as a teenager. I was lucky enough to get a deer most deer seasons, as my black friends' relations owned some acreage about 12 miles away at a small settlement named Geneva. I bought June a BB gun, and she enjoyed shooting it, but soon learned the BB's would spin off in flight and wanted something more accurate. My wife thought she might like deer hunting, so I got her a 223 caliber single shot rifle. She really surprised me on how good she could shoot.

One day I had to go get some gas for the boat so we could go fishing and one of my black friends was parked along the guard rail at Carrice Creek Bridge down on the highway and I honked the horn at him as he was unloading his tackle to fish off the bank and he waved back and on the way back from the gas station there was a wrecker and a sheriff patrol car and the deputy was arguing, it looked, because black man was pointing and moving his arms while he was talking in the deputy's face. When we came back to put the boat in the water, I noticed they were all gone. A day or two after that, I ran into him at the store and asked him about it and he said, "Yeah, they towed my van and I had to pay a ticket then pay the wrecker fee to get my van back." He argued with them because they had first put up "No Parking" signs along the bridge and he didn't notice them but would move his van but they sais it was too late he had to pay the ticket first and towed his truck anyway but he told the deputy, "They're going to find you someday." Coming home from taking June to school in the morning about a week later, I noticed skid marks on the road and someone had slid off the road at a high rate of speed and knocked all the bark off of some trees and I found out that that was my friend in his van that caused that black skid mark and crash scene and it killed him, and that didn't hardly seem right because that old van was just a way to get around and I never saw him driving it very fast. I always wondered if there wasn't some foul play there somehow.

June was now twelve years old and could go fishing and hunting with us. I remember the first youth season. She was only six years old and could shoot the 223 caliber single shot downloaded because I reloaded my own ammunition. We went early in the morning and took sandwiches and sodas and potato chips. We took a pair of deer antlers to rattle. I helped her get into the ladder stand and she started rattling those horns before it even got daylight and she would grunt on the deer call. It was a lot of fun seeing my daughter enjoy the things I liked.

When my wife went one time when June had school, the deer weren't moving so I made a huge circle on foot and pushed a spike buck right into her and she froze and couldn't shoot it, it was too innocent and too pretty. After having to be still and quiet for so long and not being able to shoot she never went again. We all did go shoot a lot and see who could do the best on a target or just show off what we could hit plinking with the 22 caliber rifles.

In the winter time June enjoyed shooting squirrels and birds with her 177 caliber pellet gun out in the yard under the trees beside the garage. June also helped me hold 2x4's in place while I was building our two-story addition. Fishing and hunting sure was a good way to get our minds off of the subdivision.

Ron Cole, the man from Oklahoma, and Paul Price came down the street one day with the maintenance men and a tractor and put steel pipes in the end of the road to block people from using the county road. These were my friends, I thought, and they were helping close up our road. My wife got so mad our friends were helping the subdivision punish the people on the house trailer side. Here they both had got put on the board of directors and were now against us. My wife told June, "That's it for the Coles. They're never going to babysit you again and you are to stay away from them." That hurt June's feelings, I know, because Mrs. Cole was closer to her than her own Grandma Curci.

I think June started hating her mom that day.

Our lawsuit was about two years old and I felt we were gaining in court but losing in the subdivision because we were getting snubbed a lot from people that used to be friendly and I didn't know why. We felt so good the district judge was on our side trying repeatedly to get the subdivision to respect the laws and bylaws and one day we got the bad news that he had apparently drowned in a swimming pool while vacationing in Mexico. They appointed a woman judge to take his place temporarily. This was only a couple of months after Andy's son-in-law was on the news as he and his wife weren't getting along and he had been arrested for being drunk. Now this was the man that threatened us with an assault weapon, and we couldn't get the law to do anything about it. When he was going to get out of jail, Andy's daughter, Nick Serrino's wife, called the sheriff's department and said she didn't want him coming home because he was a dangerous person. The sheriff followed him home and he went in and came out with a pump shotgun and began firing at the sheriff. The sheriff got behind a tree in the yard and started shooting back with his handgun after being hit in the shoulder from the shotgun. Nick never stopped coming at him and the sheriff emptied his revolver and hit Nick several times in which Nick died on the scene. Now I get the news the judge drowned and he was ten years younger than I was. All of this was just not real, it seemed.

You know, a few years before I moved to this neck of the woods, a black man was in jail in Hilltown, Texas and the deputies had let this black man out of jail to go outside and use the pay phone and beat him to death with their billy clubs. These deputies were rounded up and in prison the whole time all this was happening to us. Here we are in a beautiful setting on this planet so far away from the troubles of the big city life and all these problems all the time. My wife said, "It's just people with clout enjoying pushing other people around just because it makes themselves feel so good because of their positions." I never heard of clout before. In the subdivision all kinds of people lived there but a lot of them had a reason for being there as a heaven for them. For instance, the man that lived with a lady and her three teenage daughters was there because, being a private subdivision, he didn't have to put a sign up in his yard that he was a child molester. The one-legged fellow lived there because the law was supposed to get permission to get on the property and that let him have time to hide his drugs. One time, one-legged Tom and his friend shot his pistol up in our direction and we had to get away from the house as bullets were ricocheting all over. One day they were getting drunk over there and hollering and shouting—loud music and all. My wife said, "Watch this." She went and got our hand-held telephone and called Tom up and when he answered, my wife pretended to be an office worker in the grocery store across the lake over in Many, Louisiana and informed him he had the winning ticket to a new four wheeler they had sold sweepstakes tickets to. After the call, they were really excited and hollering "Let's go get my new four wheeler," and the little truck they were in you could hear the rods knocking in the engine and the smoke just poured out the tailpipe and they went up over the hill and out of sight, music blaring and rods knocking as they were hollering out the windows of the truck. They were so happy. Well, later towards evening they still weren't back, and we just waited to see if they would be hollering and screaming when they returned. My wife found out from a neighbor that the store had to call the police, as he wouldn't leave the store without his four wheeler he had just won. Tom spent the night in the Many jail. We could never tell about that one, but it made funny memories, and we got to secretly punish the ones that caused us so much hell.

This is the same fellow that one day, we saw him walking up the street coming towards us with a friend. He was upset and cussing all the way, and I heard him say "I'm going to kick this little one-armed son of a bitch's ass," and they continued to talk. I got up out of my chair. I told my friend to stay out of this, not say anything and just watch, and went to the back of the garage and got my 2 ½ pound sledgehammer. I came back out of the garage and headed down the driveway straight towards these fellows, because I have never been scared of the devil himself. The fellow hollered, "Shit!", and said "Let's go." They turned around and went home. I then turned around and went back to my garage, sat down with my friend and I was laughing. My friend asked me, "Why do you have 'left arm' written on the handle of the sledgehammer?", and I said "In case I have to go to court or take a lie detector test for hurting him, I can honestly say I hit him with my left arm." That seemed funny at the time, because my left arm had been removed years ago because of the motorcycle accident.

I also had trouble with Bill's brother, Sam, and he was just as crazy. At times he would come flying up to my yard, spinning tires in his little orange colored compact car, and tear up my lawn. This would make me furious, but he didn't do it very often and I was having a hard time catching him, because I was never fast enough to get out of the house and have words with him. I placed my 30-carbine at the door—a short military rifle (built for soldiers and army tanks), as it was a semi-automatic and more accurate than a 45-caliber pistol. Anyways, I saw him speeding around in the subdivision, and I got ready to greet him with my carbine, in case he should come through my place. Sure enough, here he came up the street, throwing beer cans out the window, with his radio turned up full blast. I grabbed my carbine and ran out into the yard as he came flying up the driveway, and I spread my legs and pointed my carbine into the air. He either had to run over me or stop. When I went around his front fender and got in his face, I told him "This is the last time for this bullshit!" He then called me "sir" for the first time, said he would never do it again, and that he was sorry and was just having a little fun. He and his girlfriend moved out of the subdivision. I never heard another word about him or where he went to, but he was on the news a couple of years later because a bass boat fishing in a tournament had bumped a little orange car under water in a lake over in Louisiana, just off the main road. When the wrecker called on the scene pulled the car out of the lake, Sam's body was in the car. They figured he was under water for a couple of days. Since he spent so much time drinking and drugs, he must have lost control and drove into the lake. My wife said "It's a wonder some people live as long as they do, and doing all the crazy things they do".

We found out that the fellow with Joe that day who was going to kick my ass in the driveway, was a man named Larry, and he and his wife and four little ones had nowhere to live and were staying with Joe for a few weeks at the time of the sledgehammer incident. Months later, there was a shooting in the low-rent housing in downtown Pineville on the news, and it was about Joe and Larry. Joe was cleaning a pistol and it went off, striking Larry in the chest, and he was dead on arrival at the local hospital. No charges were ever filed. It makes you wonder about that too, because Joe always bragged that one of Larry's kids was his, which put him in the driveway with Joe that day.

All these things happening about the same time and all the pressures were getting the whole family down. I was so mad and upset that one day when I was supposed to play golf, I picked up a hadite concrete block and used it for a weight for a barbell and pumped it over my head a bunch of times and shortly after that, I came down with a high fever. I was weak for a few days and then got a little better, but my right shoulder had swollen up and I could hardly use my right arm and I didn't have a left arm. They took me to Nacogdoches to get the fluid drained out with a long needle. 2 ½ cups. I remember my wife got so distraught she took June to Grandma Curci's and left here there, and went to live with her mom and stepdad. My shoulder got so bad I ended up in the hospital, and after taking lots of painkillers and antibiotics, came home for a while, and I got worse and ended up back in the hospital. I developed an open sore in my right shoulder and the doctors kept telling me it was a piece of bone trying to come out from an old motorcycle injury. After two or three months of this open hole that kept draining ugly-looking fluids, I then got so constipated from all the medicines that I ended up back in the hospital. After a couple days, I was begging the nurses to help me eat because I couldn't lift the fork to my face, and they made fun of me and said I was just wanting attention, and my wife had abandoned me because she couldn't take any more. My mom and stepfather had gone out and were able to talk my wife into coming back to me as June and I needed her so much, but after a few days the hospital called and said I was so weak I might not make it through the night. She called Mom, Mom called my brother, and he got into his car in Florida and drove nonstop to Hilltown and took me out of the hospital and drove me to a much larger hospital in Lufkin, Texas. In the emergency room, the doctor took a smear of the fluid and tested it in the lab and said, "My gosh, why haven't you been to a hospital before now?" We told him the doctor in Hilltown had been treating me for about 8 months, and after the X-ray, he said "We have to operate right away and take out your collarbone, or this osteomyelitis will kill you as most of your collarbone has already deteriorated." So now they operate and take out what's left of my collarbone on my right side, and I wake up in the hospital with my wife at my side in tears, probably thinking she'll have to take care of an invalid on top of all she has been through.

We waited for the doctor to come around in the morning, and he had me stand up and take my gown off. He explained to us what we would see under the bandage and a nurse was going to show my wife how to take the bandage off and put antibiotics on the open wound and put on a new bandage. He told my wife to brace herself, because it might shock her to see a hole full of blood and raw tissue as it had to heal from the inside out. Well, the nurse ripped the bandage off in a fast jerk, but it had stuck, so she had to do it again. The pain was immense, but when it came off my wife would have hit the floor from passing out but they expected this and a male nurse was standing close behind her and caught her as she passed out. She kept saying "No, I can't do this, I can't do this," but they said, "You are going to have to."

After that was done, the doctor asked me all about what caused this to happen to me, and I explained in short about the lawsuit and about being punished by the board members and about having to go to Nacogdoches and they used a long needle and drained 2 ½ cups of fluid from my shoulder. He then said they had probably stabbed me with a dirty needle, as they had to keep putting the same needle back in my shoulder to drain the fluids. My wife mentioned "Well, can't we sue them over this?" and he said there is no proof this is what happened, and that stress and tension does strange things to our body chemistry and that we can self-destruct over too much worry and stress. And NO, he would not help us sue, because insurance for practicing doctors is ridiculous now, and it would only help to raise premiums for fellow doctors. So here we are again, anyone can do us harm but we have no way of getting back at them. We were used to that anyway. Before going back to Hilltown, we had to wait for our medicine and get a release form from the hospital, and I needed a cigarette. I told my wife "Come on," and she said "Where are you going?" I said "To the store." She said, "We can't leave the hospital, and you're in a gown." I said "Don't worry, we'll be right back." She said "You can't drive," and I said "Sure I can." She was afraid to ride with me driving the car only hours after surgery, and it was on my right shoulder, and I had to drive with my right arm. Not only that, I even drove the 60 miles home and the first thing I did was to lift a car battery out of our boat so I could take it to the garage and charge it up so we could go fishing. The next day I played golf. I was so used to pain in my left arm, which is called phantom limb pain, so now I hurt on both sides. So what? I had endured the last two years with pain without pain medicine, so I never got used to the pain but developed a tolerance for it.

Upon returning home, we faced a new problem, but we didn't realize it right away. My wife had left our daughter with the neighbors, and they were real religious people that went to church all the time and were always talking about the Lord. We didn't have time to take June anywhere, so she ended up at the neighbors' for a couple days. The day after we got home, Mom had to answer all of June's questions about "Is Dad going to be okay?" and "Why did he get this way?" and all the questions a youngster would ask. We were so thankful that the people could, on a moment's notice, take care of our little one for us. When Mom asked June how her stay with them was, June told Mom about how they had told us that God was punishing us and that if she didn't get away from us she would be punished too and how sorry they were for her that she had to be raised by such awful parents. Here this man, Paul Smith, was the one telling me of all the bad people in the subdivision when I first moved there and all about the corruptions of the subdivision, and I thought he was my friend. Matter of fact, he was the one that mentioned I should start a petition, and he was one of the first ones to sign it. We got upset about what they told our daughter, and didn't have anything more to do with them either now. It seemed as though everyone in the whole place were backstabbers, but friends to your face. This same man was on total disability, and even got an electric chair at no charge to him and rode in it to play in our little once-a-week golf tournaments. He would turn it in for a new one about once a year because even on a short nine-hole golf course, one would only last a year. His wife had her own car for a while until he put the battery charger on his car backwards one day when the battery was dead and charged up the battery backwards and when he hooked it back up in the car it burned up the whole wiring harness. Well anyway, I found out later that even though he cut hair on the side to make extra money as a barber and she cleaned people's houses for extra money, his wife was getting money for being legally blind. She didn't even wear glasses.

Now with all this money coming in and all, now his dad dies and now they moved to the house side of the subdivision and now they look down at the trailer side, because they are important people now and can judge others. Ha.

My wife, June and I went to a garage sale and ended up trading an electric chain saw and a few other items including an old 22 rifle we didn't like and some cash for a couple Honda Passports that were only 125 cc motor bikes and only one of them would start and run and brought them home. I got them both running and June took off on hers and was jumping ditches and getting it airborne within minutes, and Mom fell down with hers on the county road and got scratched up a little but was riding it okay after bandaging up her knees and elbows. Those two had a ball on those little bikes and then I bought a 175 cc Honda dirt bike but it was too high center of gravity and neither one of them could ride that one. The year was about 97 and June was about eight years old.

When the new district judge got appointed, on the next court session the attorney against me did a summary judgment on me and I wasn't allowed to speak at the trial so we lost the lawsuit and was dealt a blow of having to pay $4000, or they would take our property away from us. The summary judgment stated that when I sold my other properties that I never paid the dues up because for record the new owners were given credit for paying the dues. This was crooked because I had knocked the dues off the price of the property, so in essence I did pay them, but the court never got a chance to hear it because the judge wouldn't let me speak.

After losing my case on a technicality and not being able to explain, I was so furious I called the local television station and they came out and made a video for the 5 o'clock and 10 o'clock news and I got my chance to speak on TV. Well, that really hit home, because after the entire viewing area got to see how corrupt things were and especially enforcing hog wire in our yard. This woman lawyer, the appointed temporary judge, was running for the district judge position. After the vote was in and after my news story about her on TV, she hardly got any votes. I then called her law office, but she was not in, so I left a message for her that Bob Thomson called and asked if she was mowing lawns and I needed my lawn mowed. I said I was the one-armed man from the subdivision she did a summary judgment on. That did me a lot of good inside for years.

My brother from Florida came here to visit because my stepdad was in the hospital with chest pains and he was the executor of the will. Well, my stepfather was only in the hospital for a couple days and they had him on life support and my brother had them pull the plug on him and we were all there at the hospital except for June, who was with a neighbor. I thought my dad was going to tear up the bed he was in because he was gasping for breath and hollering and moaning when they turned off the support. My brother met with the board of directors at the subdivision and said that my mom would pay the money for me and I would have to pay her back so much a month. My brother proposed selling me his half of the house and us selling ours and moving out of the subdivision. With the money I now owed Mom, and making her payments, making payments for the brick home too was more money than I had coming in. That made my brother so mad at us that we had refused to buy Mom's house that we hardly got any money from my stepfather's death and my brother even had a garage sale and sold off a lot of my mom and stepfather's things, and after the garage sale I could have the rest.

It ended up I had to haul the rest off to a landfill and had to pay help to do it plus pay the landfill fees. My brother went back to Florida, as it took about six months for the house to sell, and I felt so sorry for Mom because she was the big loser. She not only lost her husband, but was put in assisted living, and there was no room for her nice furniture or her belongings. During these six months, I had to drive into town almost every day and help Mom do something like wash her hair or mow the grass and paint the trim on the house and paint the garage. All the time not knowing I was going to be cheated out of my half. The house finally sold and my brother and his wife didn't want Mom too close to them, so they put her assisted living in San Angustine, Texas, about 28 miles from me.

Since the lawsuit was over, a man from the board members came over to get me to sign some important papers and I had once bought a Bronco from him that had been rolled over and it had a smashed roof and both sides were dented up and he was amazed I had put it back like new and was driving it. That was about two years before and he wasn't a board member then. Well here he was, kind of apologetic because he knew what I had been through, but nevertheless I guess he had been sent because there would be less friction. The first thing he said was, "I guess you know they want the fence up." I said "I figured that, but no hog-wire in my yard, and I want you to tell them at the meetings that I speak for the whole trailer section that we regret being referred to as 'trailer trash' openly at the meetings." He said he'd remind them not to do that, but he had no control over what people say. I told him, "We want to be called 'the gold mine.'" He said, "I don't understand. Why do you want to be called 'the gold mine'?" I said, "Look out that window and tell me what you see." He looked and said, "I see a garage and your Bronco, but I still don't get it." I said, "How big is your property?" and he said "I don't know. Maybe 180 feet by 200 feet, I guess." I said, "How much do you pay dues?" He said, "$7.50 a month." I said, "Really? Then how come we pay $7.50 for our lots, which are only 30 feet wide and 80 feet long, and all these lots only come to 80x90 feet, and my dues are $22.50 a month? Now you see why we want to be called 'the gold mine,' especially when you call us trailer trash and spend our money on the house side and won't fix our potholed, un-drivable streets. And how come you used the county road to come see me, but force me off of it?"

After he left, I went straight to the courthouse and recorded my papers of secession from the subdivision. Now that stirred them up for sure. Within 3 days, the mail lady honked the horn out at the mail box and told me there was a letter I had to sign for but she told me I didn't have to accept it. She was a former disgruntled property owner herself, so I didn't. I had made a friend of an old gentleman that fished a lot at the boat ramp while putting my boat in or out of the lake. I would talk to him occasionally about the stories of the subdivision, about the things the subdivision was doing to the people there and sort of telling on them in the letters to the editor section. He would get a kick out of them, and tell me what a good job she was doing. I found out he was a retired road commissioner and had a lot of pull downtown, so I figured he would be a good man to have on my side. One of my long-time friends had died of a heart attack, and had a young wife, but now she was going fishing a lot with Lester Butt Sr., this old gentleman. He was in his seventies and she was in her mid-thirties. This man, Mr. Butt, needed some welding done on his garden tiller, so I told him to bring it over and I'd see if we could fix it. He also had busted up his ground effects on his late-model Dodge truck and I repaired that too. He became a friend of the whole family after about a year.

With all the problems we had (and they seemed endless), my wife had so many ways of finding moments to really enjoy the little things in life. For instance, every spring when the hummingbirds would show up buzzing around, she would be one of the first to put out the hummingbird feeder and they would come back year after year and she put names on them and sometimes one particular one wouldn't come back and she feared it was killed somehow and we always had friends and neighbors come over to watch the hummingbirds light on her finger as she held her hand out of the window by the feeder. Sometimes if the feeder ran out they would come out to the garage where we would be sitting in chairs and would get right in her face and just hover at her nose as if to say, "We're out of food," and she would go fill the feeder and we would laugh about it. A few times we would see a sparrow hawk swoop down and snatch one of her little buddies right out of the air, and that was sad, but the hawk has to eat too. This bird thing wasn't only with hummingbirds. In the winter all kinds of birds came to her winter bird feeders and she even had the little chickadees also light on her fingers while she held her hand out the windows and had names for them too.

Now we had a new problem. My wife found a lump under her left armpit and was worried about it. For the last three years, I had been plagued with stomach problems, and we had been to doctor after doctor trying to get me out of pain in my stomach, but after all the other problems I just figured it was worry, and now that the doctor told me not to worry anymore because it could kill me, that went away. We ended up in Houston and they took x-rays and tests of her blood and couldn't come to any conclusion on why her thyroid gland was so huge but did tell her the knot by her navel was a ripped stomach wall and to be careful about that or it would tear worse. Here she is, all distraught about her health now. It seemed like it was just one thing after another. Since I was on VA disability, we didn't have health insurance, and no money to keep going to doctors. She said she was okay, but you knew she wasn't. Can you imagine what our daughter must have thought in her mind about her parents' problems?

Back when June was only three years old, I drew a rabbit on a sheet of paper, and she was so amazed she asked me if she could do that. I said, "This is the United States of America and we are free to do anything we want as long as it doesn't break any laws." From that day on she started drawing animals and farm scenery. In the third grade, they held their yearly Deerfest and gave prizes for all kinds of events and in school they gave all the kids colored pencils and paper, and said "See how good you can do in an art contest." June drew a scene with a pond and sunset, and it had a buck and a doe and a sunset and it won first place and they called us up and told us she had won a four-wheeler, but instead it was a three-foot-tall trophy with her name and class on it. She sure was proud of that, and we were too. June never talked about boys or wanted to go spend the night with girlfriends or anything. All she wanted was to stay in her room and draw. She got to drawing hundreds of horses and listening to oldie goldie music all the time.

All these problems never stopped us from fishing. We always had time for that, except in winter when it got cold, but that's when we hunted. Mom didn't go anymore, but June did, on weekends when there wasn't any school. We also went to Natchitoches, Louisiana, every New Year's for the fireworks and every Fourth of July, which was our wedding anniversary. Barb even wanted to trade her four-wheeler for a huge flat-bottomed boat a friend of ours had, so we did, and I put a 20-horsepower electric start motor on it. It was 18 feet long and was 6 feet wide inside. What a boat. We really had fun in that now. It was so roomy, and you could stand up and walk around in it. We even started to bait out holes in the lake and catch huge catfish on rods and reels. We got used to getting our line broken on the big ones, as the lake was full of submerged trees. The big ones would strip out line and make it into the trees, and it would wrap around them and break off. June loved bringing them back as far as the boat ramp and giving them away to black people fishing on the bank. I remember one time, while fishing in the deep part of the old riverbed, we hadn't been anchored up for more than fifteen minutes, and just got all the poles baited with live bream and all of the poles (at least four of them) all started pulling at the same time. Barb got her catfish in, and I was holding a pole with my foot as June was pulling on one and I was too. Barb ran back to the pole that I was holding, and I heard a loud bang, and I didn't know what that was, but Barb was pulling in another one and as I brought mine in the boat and was trying to keep it from sticking a fin in Barb's foot, I saw what had made that loud noise. One of the large top water lures that was hanging loose on one of the bass poles lying on the floor of the boat had snagged Barb's little toe as she ran to the back of the boat. The treble hook was embedded under the toenail of her little toe. The loud snap was when the line stretched tight and eventually broke. We used 20 pound test line. I knew she was in a lot of pain, because the end of her little toe was a lot whiter than the rest of the toe. I got a pair of pliers and tried jerking it out backwards, but the large hooks had strong barbs, so I said, "Okay. I'm taking you to the doctor." We threw the rest of the poles over to one side and I cranked up the 18-foot-long flat-bottom and took off, and in my haste I forgot about the anchor. I had the 20-horsepower outboard wide open, and the boat made a circle, and June hollered "Hey Dad, the anchor is still out!" and I said "Yeah, I know, I was just about to get around to that," and we all laughed, but I had wound the rope around something and had to cut the rope and lose the anchor. Even though Barb was in a lot of pain, she even laughed at the tight circle the boat made, like a carnival ride, or something fun. It kind of took our minds off the fish hook for a second. I raced back, and by the time we got to the boat ramp (about 1 ½ miles), Barb had pulled at the hook until it ripped out meat and all against the barb.

I spent a lot of time on different trucks, cars and a van because my wife was always wanting to get a different car or truck and I had to make it perfect for her with a new paint job and fancy it up before she traded for another one. Every year I would dig up the garden spot and turn it by hand with a shovel in February and fertilize it so we could enjoy some home-grown vegetables. In East Texas, in the wintertime, Lester Butt Sr. would come by and get me to ride with him as we would be looking for deer dogs to shoot because deer dogs were illegal and he hated them because hunters would turn their dogs loose on his properties and the dogs would run the deer that he was feeding off of his property and the hunters would shoot them in the forest neighboring his property. We did this a number of times, but never did shoot not even one dog. Instead, we went to cafes and coffee shops where he would talk politics and run down the men running for office against his son who was running for

J. P. I knew one of the men he was talking about, and my daughter went to school with his daughter. Lester would say, "My God, anyone that would sleep with their own daughter ought to be hung." I hated to be around him making such accusations, because I knew he was making it up to make sure his son won the election. Nevertheless, I just tried to change the subject or would just be quiet. I never was much for politics.

I sure was glad LHPOA wasn't bothering us anymore.

June and Mom would ride their Honda Passports all over the subdivision, and June even got to ride at times without Mom. June came home one day and told how a dog ran out and tripped the bike and she went down, but didn't get hurt. Another day one of the lesbian women that lived on the house side stopped June and gave her a big hug and kiss on the lips, and told June, "We think so much of you and love you, but you can't help your parents are the way they are." June said the lady got her lips wet with her saliva. Mom got furious again and told June she wasn't to go on the house side ever again. It seemed like every time we tried to do right, it punished June even more. The only place to ride on a smooth road was on the house side. What a deal. I felt sorry for June, but Mom was right, I thought. Maybe that's why June just stayed in her room and drew horses all the time and listened to oldie goldie music.

One day Lester's tiller's chain came off and it was stretched to the point it wouldn't adjust, so I took it apart and took a link out of the chain and one of his friends stopped to talk to Lester and also wanted to meet me. His name was Augie, and he had the last name of Stanish. He was married, but separated. June was out in the yard and came over to see who else was here and they were introduced. June had started filling out as a young lady and was a pretty girl. Augie hugged her and told her how pretty she was and how lucky Mom and Dad are to have such a pretty daughter.

This guy Augie had his share of charisma to make everyone feel good, while he hugged our daughter for a few more seconds than needed. A red flag should have been thrown, because this guy was just too friendly. Lester and Augie loaded up Lester's tiller and Lester left, but Augie wanted to see my little body shop and he said he buys and sells and swaps all kinds of stuff in need of repair and painting and he could make it worth while for me to do some work for him occasionally. I said "Yeah, we can do that," but it bothered me he couldn't keep his eye off of June, because he was 46 years old and June just turned 13.

Augie told me we'd have to come down to his houseboat sometime, and we'd fish off of his houseboat. He said it was a large houseboat on top of two huge propane tanks for pontoons, and each one had its own motor in the back part of the tank, both being 6-cylinder Chevy truck engines that hadn't been run in a long time. Maybe I could help him tune them up. My wife said "No, I think we should stay away from that guy." I guess another month passed before he stopped at my garden where I was tilling with a shovel. Anyway, he wanted for me to meet his wife, and she seemed pretty and nice, and they went on their way.

It was now the time when the crappie were in, and we did love to eat crappie. About a week later, Augie stopped again and said "Y'all gotta come down to my place. The crappie are biting like crazy." Well, we couldn't resist, and we all went down. He had a huge houseboat with its own generator for lights, and it was also hooked up to a power pole. He built it with a large hole in the middle of the floor which could be lifted up to fish while watching TV and still be by the fireplace. Really nice. This was in the spring of 2003. We made good friends and enjoyed playing Texas Hold'Em poker as we watched the crappie pull on the fishing poles and would take the fish off, put him in the cooler, and wash our hands and go back to playing cards. Sometimes we even cooked shrimp or crappie at the same time.

Augie always showed off a wallet that was thick with hundred-dollar bills, but he did not have a job. He did run trot lines and sold catfish all over Texas. He ran not only his trot lines, but everyone else's. He always had lots of catfish to clean. He had just bought a used Dodge dually one-ton truck, and was proud of it. It sure was nice, with the subdivision leaving us alone. We all did our own thing, till Tuesday evening when Augie would come over or we would go to his place and play Texas Hold'Em and cook. I tuned up his motors and I painted another large propane tank for him out on the edge of the county road, but he kept stringing me along. Every time I was to get paid, he would want to trade me something that didn't run or didn't work, but it got him out of paying me cash. He was real good pals with Lester's son, as he was the Justice of the Peace now, and I went over there to his house with Augie several times. His name was Jake Butt and Augie bragged about being one of the chosen few who had his home telephone number, which was 0001. I don't know if it was true or not, but Augie told me there were several people that would give Jake boats, welders, generators and all kinds of items to get off the hook for their

DWIs and different charges if Jake would take care of it for them, and Augie would end up selling them or trading other items for them. They kind of had a little business on the side, so to speak. It sure looked that way. The more I learned about the law in that town, the more I didn't want to know. June was only 13, but a lot of the time she would be a big winner because you never knew when she was bluffing or not when playing Texas Hold'Em.

My wife spent a lot of time worrying about her hernia and the lump under her arm. Actually, it was in her left armpit. She liked to walk the county road for exercise, and occasionally I would go with her and we would just walk and talk. Sometimes we would walk right up on some deer or have them cross the road not far from us. That would always be an exciting moment. These walks would be while June was in school. Life was starting to be a little easier without so many problems except for Barb not wanting to do any more about her lumps and bumps. She was doing a lot of reading and studying health books to try and figure it out herself, and she was the one that fixed my ulcer problem. She bought a book that was called *Foods That Harm and Foods That Heal* and said if I ate raw cabbage, it would fix my ulcers. After eating raw cabbage for a couple weeks, I was better, and after a couple months, I forgot I had a problem.

Without the crappie spawning, we only saw Augie on Tuesday nights, but enjoyed it. He would always bring us some shrimp or crappie to cook or we would cook at his houseboat. As the subdivision had taken the pressure off of us, I had more body and paint work, and everything seemed to be on the mend. One day in the summer of 2004, Lester picked up June and I, and we were going somewhere, I don't remember, but he asked June if she would be able to go to the stock car races in Many, Louisiana. His other son, LJ they called him, raced a stock car on a quarter mile dirt track. June said "No, Mom don't let me go nowhere." Lester said, "If I was you, I'd put a bullet in her damn head." I couldn't believe he would tell her something like that. She said, "You can't do that! You would end up in prison!" Lester said, "Ah, no, baby doll, I'd never let them do that to you. Don't you worry about that one damn bit." It kind of shocked me that he would say something like that, but it didn't rattle me because old men are bold and say things to impress people. I just shook my head at June in disgust and didn't say a word. Here is an old man with diabetes and all kinds of old age problems talking like he is some big shot to a teenager. I didn't even tell my wife about it, because she would have thrown a fit and jumped on June, and it would have just been more bad memories.

About a week later, Lester's wife called us and was real nice and asked us if June could go to the stock car races with them, and I said "Let me talk it over with my wife and we'll see." We talked it over and decided that as long as she was with them, it would be okay. They promised us June would ride with them and they would bring her home. They did say Augie would probably come and sit with them, because he usually went too in his own truck. They came and picked her up and everything seemed okay. June had never been on a date yet because she was only 13 years old. She had never been interested in any boy or talked about any boys yet. They were supposed to be back shortly after midnight, because the races were usually over by 11 PM.

September 2nd was just another day, this was the day before June went to the races, and since it was the day after payday, we went shopping at the Wal-Mart in Many, Louisiana. Mom and June went their separate ways. June usually went to the art supplies, because now she was into painting with brushes and paint instead of colored pencils, and Mom was gathering up cleaning supplies and such for the house. I usually went to check out the fishing and hunting goods. I had traded off her .22 rifle because it had a clip and only held seven rounds and the clip was hard to load on the fingers, and I found one on sale that had a tubular magazine, just what I was wanting, because we all would shoot it. After getting home, I found out why it was probably on sale. The back sight was about to fall out and probably a flaw from manufacturing. Anyway, I tried to hammer on the barrel to tighten up the dovetail and it didn't work after several tries so I decided to mix some JB weld (liquid metal) and glue the rear sight in place. It was quite an effort, because it takes about a half hour to start setting up and 24 hours to get really hard. I did this out in the sunshine so it would set up faster. The only thing is if it would get hard without being in the right place, the gun wouldn't shoot on the center of the target. The way I handled this was to put it close and wait till the weld started to get rubbery and make any final adjustments by shooting it in as it hardened. It was kind of a family event, since we all got to shoot it before it was completely hard while I could still move the sight left or right. So we then just left it loaded on a chair in the garage so as not to disturb or bump the gun as the epoxy glue hardened. If it didn't harden in the right place, it was easy to cut off with a knife, but after 24 hours, it was permanent. After a couple hours,

I shot it a couple times more and it was going to be okay. I let June and Mom practice loading and unloading and using the safety and all to be familiar and get to know the rifle to be safe handling it while shooting it. June was amazed at how many cartridges it would hold and shot it well, as did Mom.

I locked up the garage after shooting the last few times and put it on pillows on a chair in the garage and made sure the gun was level or gravity would shift the sight while hardening. That was a job but better than taking it back and explaining or doing paperwork to return it. I remembered June asking me if a .22 can kill a deer, and I said, "Heck, yeah. The bullet will go clean through a deer's head."

It was September 3, 2004, and my wife and I watched TV till late and it became 12 PM and my wife and I were anxious to hear about the good time at the races. About 15 minutes to one AM, my wife couldn't stand it any longer and called Lester's home phone and asked why didn't they drop June off, as they lived six miles past our house. They told us they had let Augie bring her home because he had to go right by our house. My wife threw a fit and said they'd better get here pretty damn quick, and hung up. When it got to be 2 AM, my wife called again and said, "They're not here yet," and that's when Lester got on the phone and said there were some extra races they didn't stay for, but maybe June and Augie stayed until they were through, and my wife and I went out to the county road to watch for headlights coming up the road. My wife came in and called Lester one more time, and this time they hung up on my wife and said not to call them any more that night. Here my wife and I were, back on the dirt county road, sitting, waiting and watching for Augie's dually to come towards us on the county road, about 2:30 AM or 3 AM. We could hear a vehicle coming ¾ mile away, because the road was so bad it usually stayed like a washboard in between gradings. Now we could see the headlights and it seemed to be speeding towards us. It didn't hit the brakes till it got to us, and it was Augie and June. I'm sure they could see us standing out in the road from a quarter of a mile away. When it stopped, June jumped out, and there was no time to say anything to Augie as he spun tires leaving in that big diesel dually.

Mom said, "June, where have you been? Get in that house this very minute, young lady, you've got some explaining to do." My wife just kept hollering at June all the way to the door and June kept hollering back, "OK, Mom, OK, Mom, OK, Mom, settle down. It's OK. It's OK. I'm home."

My wife was so upset. I had never seen her this way before. I knew she had always been a little overprotective of our daughter, but I understood why after hearing how she was molested and mistreated as a child herself. My wife did not ever hit June, nor did she this night after all of this, and I was feeling sorry for June because Mom just kept hollering at her and telling her she was grounded and not to ask for anything, or to go anywhere until she said it was OK. She just kept saying "Where have you been and what have you been doing all this time? Lester and his wife have been home for two hours and they were supposed to bring you home. How did you get with Augie and what have you been doing?" I tried to calm my wife down and she jumped all over me verbally and said she could handle this. If June had been a boy, it would have been my job, but since she was a girl she wanted to handle it. I tried once more a few minutes later, as my wife just seemed out of control over her own emotions, she was so shook up. Now she told me, "Go do something or go outside and smoke a cigarette, but just let me get a few things straight with our thirteen-year-old grown-up daughter, here."

I went outside, hoping that it would end soon. I didn't realize that June might take this as me being a traitor to her. From what I found out later, I guess my wife was shoving June up against the dining room wall to make June look her in the face, and the last thing I heard my wife say was, "If I ever catch you around that child molester again, I'll kill you—you understand me?" I was outside and Mom said a few more things where I couldn't hear what she said, but as I entered the dining room, she told June "Now get ready for bed. I've had enough for one day." June didn't say a word, but disappeared in a hurry.

Early September nights in Texas were sometimes in the mid 80-degree range, and this night was no exception. I went upstairs to bed and was so glad this was all over. I had opened the windows and let the breeze come through the upstairs bedroom hours before, because it was not going to be long until the sun would come up. I have always been an early riser, and by now I had been up for about 20 hours and was pooped out with all the commotion for the last three or four hours. I got undressed and just dropped on the bed. It probably didn't take me long to fall fast asleep. Since it was so hot, I usually slept naked, as no one could walk in the room since it was upstairs.

I awoke to hear screaming and crying and sobbing, and it was June coming up the stairs. I hollered "What's wrong?" and June said, "Come quick, Dad, I think Mom's been shot." At first I ran to the dresser drawers to get some underwear, but putting my hand on the dresser and feeling for the handle I thought, "What if she's on her last breath? She wasn't making a sound." I just thought, "June will just have to not look." I felt I didn't have time to go across the room to the light switch and come back and get dressed. I ran down the stairs and Mom was lying on the couch moaning, and there was blood all over her pillow. I didn't remember saying anything, but remember the deep pain in my body of fright. I started to move her head to one side but couldn't see any wound, but there was a lot of blood everywhere and it was already dark and puddled. I turned around and called 911 and told the police to get an ambulance here fast, because I thought my wife had been shot.

I ran upstairs and got dressed and came back down and called Greg, a friend of mine that had been working with me helping me do body work and paint cars of his that he would sell. He was Augie's next-door neighbor, and had just moved in about a month ago. Greg and his wife got there in less than five minutes, and were also shocked that something like this had just happened to us.

We asked June if she had seen or heard anything. She said she heard a loud bang, and when she came in the living room, Mom was lying on the couch moaning, and she came and got me. She said later, when she went to the bathroom, she noticed the back door to the house trailer was wide open and there was a gun lying in between the house and the back step. I went and looked for the gun, didn't see it, and came back to listen to Greg's wife and her questions and June's answers. Town was about 15 miles away, so we at first were patiently waiting for the ambulance, but after about 15 or 20 minutes I called again, and by now I was really getting shook as Mom needed attention right this minute, and I thought she might expire before they could get there. Greg kept saying, "Where in the hell are they? I'd hate to be in need of an ambulance around here." I called them again and the dispatcher said, "They're on their way, be patient." I said, "How can I be patient when my wife may be dying in front of me?"

I tried to talk to her again and she was just moaning and when I tried to turn her head to get a better look, there was a puddle of blood on both sides of her head, and one eye was pointed a different direction. I thought, "Oh, my God, she is really bad. I hope they get here soon. What is keeping them? It's unbelievable this is happening!"

The ambulance finally pulled up and stopped, as I had told them they couldn't miss the place, all the lights were on and the rest of the neighborhood was pitch dark. The ambulance was a diesel truck and the windows were up and they just sat there in the middle of the county road. I ran to them and said "Please hurry, it's my wife." They couldn't hear me because their windows were rolled up. I motioned to them to roll the window down, but the driver just held up one finger, as if to say "Just one minute." Greg came over and called to him, "You dumb son of a bitch, you got the right place. There's a lady dying in there. What's wrong with you people?" I ran back into the house and called 911 again and told them "The ambulance is here, but they won't get out of the truck. Can you please call them and tell them they are at the right place and to come help my wife?" The dispatcher told me that when there is a shooting involved, they weren't allowed to do anything until the law got there.

While I was talking to her, a deputy came in the house, so I hung up. I told him, "OK, you're here. Can you please tell the guys in that ambulance to come help my wife?" He said, "Yes, in a moment, first tell me what happened here." I said, "I don't know yet, but I do know my wife needs help right now!" Within the next few minutes, there were at least 8 deputies all over the house, moving around, looking under beds, in closets, even in drawers. June and I were standing at the dining room table being questioned as the others were looking at everything in the house. Greg and his wife were outside standing by the garage. The emergency team of two men came in with a stretcher and let my wife's head just hang down as they dragged her off the couch. I thought, "How unprofessional is this?"

They took her out to the ambulance and it just sat there. I asked the deputy, "Why aren't they rushing her to the hospital?" He said, "I guess they have to administer immediate first aid. Not to worry. I'm sure they're doing the best they can do." I went outside to thank Greg for coming over, and he said "No problem. Glad I could help."

It was still dark outside, and I heard June hollering "Dad, Dad, look what I found out in the garden!" She was holding our new rifle and walking towards me to give it to me. I said, "June, you shouldn't be touching that," and took it from her using only my thumb and one finger on the front sight. I took it in the dining room and placed it in a corner of the room just outside the door. Two of the deputies came over, and one picked it up and took it in the kitchen and took the tube out of the magazine and poured all of the shells out on the little cutting board table in the kitchen. I noticed a whole pile of .22 shells come out of it, and some rolled off the table on the floor. The other deputy picked them up and put them back in the pile. Three different deputies took turns and looked the rifle over before throwing it on top of the spare tire in the trunk of a deputy's car. It kind of got me, him dropping it on a metal wheel when I am so particular about my guns, but I had a lot more things to worry about than a little thing like that.

It was getting a little lighter in the sky, as it would soon be dawn, and the ambulance was still sitting there. The chief of police walked up to me and asked me if I minded if he would tape off my place and call it an attempted homicide, and I said, "Of course not. Do what you have to do." They put their plastic ribbon around the whole property, and it was yellow plastic tape that said "CRIME SCENE NO TRESPASSING." The ambulance finally left, and I felt a little better that they were finally going to do something. He told me I wouldn't be allowed back in until the place was investigated. He also told me they had airflighted my wife to either Houston or Shreveport, but didn't know which one yet. One deputy found $70 in a vase on top of the radio, and asked me whose money it was. I said, "I guess my wife had a secret stash I didn't know about." I put it in my wallet because I was going to need it for gasoline.

June and I put on good clothes and headed out to Houston, but as I got down to the highway, there was the ambulance out in a field beside a helicopter. I stopped and asked the chief of police, "Where do I go?" He said, "They have changed and are going to Shreveport hospital." I asked him, "Is my wife still here?" and he said "Yes, but she'll be leaving soon."

Shreveport was 90 miles away, and I guess I cried most of the way, and was telling June she was really going to have to help me with Mom. Who knew, she might die or even be an invalid or blind. June never cried or looked discouraged. She was just quiet as we listened to the radio and settled in for the drive. We stopped for gas at the first station I came to, because the 1986 Chevy van was a V-8 engine and only got about 15 mpg. Shortly after being on the road, it got daylight.

When we got to the hospital, we parked the van and went inside, but no one knew where she was and I thought we might be at the wrong hospital. They said "No, this is where they came, but she is not in a room yet." June and I went to the cafeteria to get something to eat and drink for breakfast and there were policemen everywhere. I remember thinking, "They sure have a lot of security in this hospital." We ate and put our trays up and were walking out of the dining area, and about four or five policemen grabbed me and told me I was under arrest. I said, "Wait a minute, I haven't done anything! I want to find out who did this just as much or more than you do." They immediately saw I wasn't resisting or trying to run, and said, "OK, come with us." We went to a room that had "Security" on the door and they told June to have a seat and took me in another room and there was a Texas Ranger and he said, "Sit down, I have to ask you some questions."

I don't remember all the questions, but I couldn't help him much. He couldn't understand why the gunshot didn't wake me up. I didn't think to tell him then, but even lightning doesn't wake me up if I'm sound asleep. Then after about 15 or 20 minutes, it was June's turn, and I had to wait for her. We were then told to hang around and not go anywhere. I did call my mom in the rest home and tried to tell her, but I couldn't hardly make sense because I was crying so much.

We stayed all day and didn't get to see her because she was in ICU, and we stayed all night and slept in chairs in the waiting room. We stayed for a short time in the morning and after talking to the doctors they said it would probably be a few days before we'd get to see her—she was really bad. She was put on life support in the ambulance and in the helicopter, and now in the hospital. June and I headed back to Hilltown, and when we got home the tape was still around the trailer. Augie pulled up and got out, and June went running to his arms. He lifted her up off the ground and they were both smiling and happy. That pissed me off. Then the dog jumped up in June's arms, and Augie just kept holding June off the ground, and I said, "Well, aren't you going to turn loose?" June dropped the dog, but he kept holding June. I gave them a hard look and said, "I didn't mean the dog," and Augie let June down.

Augie said, "Have y'all eaten?" and June said no. He said, "Let's go to the store, and I'll buy." June said "Sure, Dad, let's go." I really didn't want to go, but we couldn't get in the house yet, and it was killing me. We went into the supermarket, and everyone there knew us, and June and Augie were acting too happy and all smiles. I had to remind them, "I don't know how y'all can be so happy when Mom is in intensive care and may not live." They got straight faced, but snickered at each other not knowing I was watching. 2 + 2 has always equaled 4 in my book, and my heart sunk as I realized what must have happened to June's mother, my wife. Those two lovebirds knew exactly what happened.

I had to leave June at a friend of my wife's, who lived in a nearby farmhouse not far from our house but not in the subdivision. She was an elderly lady, but still got around good. I told June I was going back to Shreveport, but I didn't. I stayed at home and ran around and did some investigating on my own. Greg had found out that his neighbor, Jim, and his wife had seen Augie coming home the back way in a real hurry around 4 AM the morning my wife got shot. That led me to believe Augie did the shooting. I couldn't bring myself to believe my daughter could be so cold-hearted as to shoot her own Mom while she was asleep on the couch, and maybe he knew how to keep the gun from making a loud bang. Now that I was coming out of shock and starting to put the pieces together, there were lots of things that didn't make any sense to me. One thing that bothered me, and still does, is the fact that there were so many deputies going through everything before the investigation, and why didn't they wear rubber gloves? They had handled every doorknob, piece of furniture, even took turns handling the rifle without gloves. How many were involved in getting rid of my wife?

I went to talk to the judge and told him what I thought, and he said, "Tell the sheriff—I'm the judge. I don't need to hear this." I was upset. I thought the judge would help because he was my wife's friend and former schoolteacher. I didn't want to go to the sheriff, because the JP hung out at the jail and he was friends with all the deputies and was Augie's best friend. I even had and still have thoughts—did someone back out? Was I supposed to get a bullet too? I guess I'll never know. I never was good at figuring out mystery movies.

I hid the van and never turned on the lights for a couple nights, as I was supposed to be in Shreveport. I was calling Shreveport hospital every morning, early, and every night hoping to find out if she would be able to make it, but all I ever got was that she was still on the critical list and not allowed visitors.

When this happened, Greg and I were in the middle of restoring an old Chevy pickup for a friend of his dad's, so we worked on it every day as it was full of dents. I know a lot of people probably thought I was terrible not being at the hospital, but there wasn't any sense in sitting in a waiting room in a seat and not being allowed to see her. Besides, working kept my mind from feeling sorry for myself and hurting worse. I did go back to the hospital a couple times, and after two weeks, the hospital finally called and said I needed to come pay my respects to my wife, because it had been too long, and that they were going to have to discontinue the life support. June did not want to go, so I went and got my mom to go with me.

Without a doubt, these were the worst days of my life. I signed all the papers and went and talked to her and let her know I would always love her and I would get to the bottom of this for her. I then kissed her on the shoulder and she was cold. We then left for San Angustine. In the meantime, Nadel Jones, the lady that kept June, called me after I acted like I came home and picked her up and said that June made her take her down to Augie's houseboat to leave an envelope in his mailbox. I called Greg and talked to him about what was going on and what I had found out, and they proposed a pizza party for June and their two little girls June's age, and at the party they would try to get on June's side and get her to talking to get it off her chest and come clean.

I had already told June if she did it and didn't confess, she would probably go to prison, but if she did and they found out it would really be bad. She said, "Don't worry, Dad, I didn't do it." I believed in her so much that I thought, well, it had to be Augie.

We had the party and I just dropped her off. About an hour later, I called, and she was having a great time, and I said "OK, just checking on you," and she said "OK, Dad, I'm fine." Two hours later, Greg's wife called and said "You'd better call the sheriff. June just told us all about it and she is crying on my bed now." I said, "You mean June shot Barb?" She said "Yep—she told us all about her and Augie going parking, and denied making love to him, but he did hurt her down there with his big fingers."

I called the sheriff, and June was arrested. That really hurt me, and they wouldn't let me be in the room when she wrote her statement or even listen to the confession on a tape recorder. Now I was hurting even worse, because now I had not only lost my wife, but my daughter too. What I remember the most about this time of my life is that it didn't matter if I wore my prescription glasses or not, because my eyes were so full of tears that I couldn't even focus for hours at a time, and I would find myself moaning and breathing deep with pain from heartache.

June was kept in detention in Lufkin, and only me or my mom could visit. They had me sign papers for permission for her to take stomach medicine. I guess she was having a lot of trouble with her stomach now, with all the worry. Every time I called, she would not talk to me. The state had got her a lawyer, and he told her not to talk to me. Here again, I thought I was doing the right thing, but got punished even more. She was there for about a month when she finally said I could come and visit, so I picked up Mom and we drove the 60 miles to see her, and when we got there, she had changed her mind.

Mom kept asking me if I believed she did it, and I would say "No, I think she is covering for Augie." She would say, "I don't think she did it either." Mom said, "Now what are you going to do?" I said, "Mom, I'm blank. I don't know. I just can't answer that question right now." After that, when some of the neighbors would see I was at home, they would knock on the door and I would let them in and I would get hugs and they would tell me how sorry they felt for me and ask all kinds of questions, and it made me feel so good to have so many friends. That was just people being nosy. After they left, they never had anything to do with me anymore. Then I heard how they had twisted up to tell others what they had found out from me. This came from friends who would bring back to me what was being said about the things that had happened. Life sure can be a bummer sometimes.

I called the judge and made an appointment with him to talk about Augie molesting June, and when I got to the courthouse and went up to the judge's office, Jake Butt, the JP who was Augie's friend, moved a chair over beside the judge's desk and said to have a seat as he closed the door. The judge asked me, "How can I help you?" and I said, "I would like to have Augie Stanish arrested for molesting a minor, my daughter." They both sat there and told me I couldn't do that because it was up to June. If she didn't complain, I couldn't do anything about it. I argued with them that it was on her confession, and that I was her father and she was a minor. It was frustrating to have the judge and JP sit there and tell me I couldn't do anything about it. I left there mad and frustrated, so the next day I drove to Lufkin and went to the FBI and told them my story, and he went out of the room for a few minutes, and came back and told me that he sympathized with me, but he flat out told me that one thing the FBI doesn't do is mess with elected officials, and that ended that.

The next day, I drove all the way down to Texas down by Houston and tried to find Sherry, Augie's wife. I went to Augie's rented property and talked to his tenants, and they told me all kinds of tales of Augie's troubles in that town and that to find Sherry I might try asking at the newspaper office because the tenant knew one of her friends owned the newspaper. I went there and the owner wasn't there, but they called him on his cell phone and said he would be right there. We talked for a while and I told him about Augie and my daughter, and it didn't surprise him one bit. He didn't have a good word for Augie. He said he couldn't give me Sherry's phone number or address, but he would take mine and give it to her and she would call me.

She did call, and we talked for a long time, and she told me she and Augie hadn't been married long before she found out so much about him she wouldn't even change her last name over to his and wanted a divorce right away, but Augie wouldn't even talk to the lawyer. Augie had gotten caught up with by the IRS and had married a woman not long ago to pay his back taxes and got a divorce and married Sherry soon afterwards. She said he owned several properties but had nothing in his own name, not even his truck. She said he had been in trouble with young girls before. The more I learned, the more I realized how much of an optimist he was and a user of everyone around him. Now I realize he had just used the JP and the judge and June to get my daughter, and my wife and I got in his way. I believe the JP and the judge got in too deep and had to ruin my wife and I in order to cover up everything and get June off the hook.

When June's hearing came, I thought I would be able to see her, but I wasn't allowed in. What was this? She was my daughter! I tried to get in, but Augie was there. He got to go in, but I didn't. I was taken to the basement of the courthouse and frisked for knives and guns in my pocket. Augie and Lester knew I had one of those little .22 caliber North American pistols that would fit in a cigarette pack. I think it was about 3 months since she was arrested. She finally got her day in court, and I wasn't allowed in. I did get questioned by her attorney in court, but was barred from the rest of it. Court lasted two days, and I ran into Augie's wife Sherry. She was there for court. It sure made for some big eyes as we ate lunch together in the same cafeteria with the attorneys and the people that worked in the courthouse.

I ran into the chief of police, and he said, "I need to talk to you outside." Once outside, he jumped all over me for going to the FBI, and said "Why did you do that? We have everything under control here and that was not a good thing to do." He acted like he would arrest me if I did it again. After court, the jury went into deliberation, and I had been in touch with June's probation officer, and he was a very down-to-earth and understanding man. As we awaited the verdict, I sat there worrying, but kept being distracted from my thoughts by all the laughter and shouting in the jury's room for deliberation. Instead of a quiet room and sorrow, or whatever you would call it, it sounded like a New Year's party, with everyone celebrating something, and it went on for 2 ½ hours. It got to be late, and I had been there all day without anything to eat, so I asked if it was all right to go get a burger, and they said go ahead.

When I was on the way up the stairs, I met the judge on the way out. I said, "Are they through?" and he said, "You're going to be a happy dad." I ran the rest of the way and burst into the courtroom and everyone was gathering up their stuff getting ready to go home and everyone was smiling. Someone came to me and said, "They found her not guilty." I ran to June and she let me hug her and I said, "Let's go home." She said "OK," but the juvenile probation people came over to me and said, "Well, don't you have to get her room ready and get the house ready for her homecoming?" I said "No, everything is clean and in order. She can come home tonight." Then they said, "Well, we think it would be best if she went with us tonight, and she can come home tomorrow. That will give you time to get used to the idea of her coming home, and she can get her stuff together." They were so persistent that I finally said "Well, OK, I guess, but if she wants she can come home now." They said "Tomorrow." I said "OK." Here I was, in shock again, but in a good way now. I was so glad it was over.

Well, the next day I called the judge and he told me they had put June in a foster family and that I should be patient, and I would get her back soon. I was patient, but I couldn't understand why we couldn't at least talk on the phone. A few days went by, and I called the juvenile probation officer, and he said "Just be patient." That scared me because maybe they were looking at me now. I did get the sheriff to give Augie a lie detector test.

One day, when I answered the phone, it was June. She was all excited and said not to tell anyone she called me, but that she was on a farm down by Jasper, Texas, and she was living with some of her lawyer's friends and that she borrowed the cell phone she was on and no one knew she was calling me. The foster parents had taken her and some other foster kids out to this farm so they could ride horses and left them there at another man's farm. She said they wouldn't ever let her call me, and that the foster parents smoked pot and partied and got drunk, and that it was terrible there and that she was being held there against her will. I said, "What do you want me to do?" She said to call Bill, the chief of police, and see if he couldn't do something. I said, "OK, I'll be in touch. Call me when you can." She said "OK" and hung up.

I called Bill and he said "No, the state put her there, and she's not being held against her will." I then told him about the pot and beer drinking. He said, "I don't know about that now." A few days later I got a call from the foster parent, and he said, "You can come get your daughter if you want because we think it would be better if she was with her own dad, and she wants to come home so bad. We will make it straight with everyone else." I said, "OK. When?" He said "Tomorrow. Call me and we'll meet someplace." I said, "OK." I couldn't hardly wait for the sun to come up. I called, and they told me a little convenience store on a certain street, and they would be there at eleven o'clock. I said "OK, I'm on the way." I thought I wasn't going to make it on time, because I had run the wheels off of my little Nissan truck and overheated it as it must have had a plugged radiator. I was running special additive in the antifreeze because it was a recurring problem. I had to pull over at a bridge, and I found a paper cup from a large fountain drink, and had to make several trips down to the water at Sam Rayburn Lake to fill the radiator up and was back up to speed.

When I got there at the store, they weren't there. A police car kept circling the block and another came into the store, got a soda and left. After a while, the phone rang at the store and it was June's foster dad. He said something came up and they couldn't make it. I called the juvenile probation office and told him what was going on and he said to stay right there, he was going to call June's lawyer. I waited about an hour, and a deputy showed up and told me to follow him to the police department. They asked me what this was all about, and I explained it to him, and he said "Just sit and I'll see what's going on." The probation officer called the police station and told me I needed to go home, they couldn't give her to me. Now what was I going to do??? I went home and was really upset, but nothing had made sense in so long that this was par.

After I got back to Hilltown, the foster parents called me and said that to give her back I would have to go to Child Protective Services and they would bring her back. I called CPS and had to drive to St. Angustine, Texas, and fill out all kinds of forms to get her back. A few days later I got a call that I could go get my daughter in Jasper. This time I met them and we went to a car dealership and they had some papers notarized and gave June to me and the people didn't even care to talk or say goodbye to June, just burnt rubber leaving in a hurry. The CPS lady said I was to report to her when I got June and bring her with me. We did that and the lady got real smart with June and said she was a lucky girl to be able to be with me and that June needed to straighten up her act. I though the lady was acting big because of her position at that time, or else she knew something I didn't. Since St. Angustine's CPS office was only about a mile and a half from where Mom was, we went and surprised her too. My mom, who was about 84 years old, was really happy for us to get June back. I asked June why her glasses were so crooked, and she said the foster parents had backhanded her and bent them up. It was time for a new pair anyway. I was continuously having to buy her medicine for her stomach too.

I put June back in school and a lot of the students wouldn't talk to her, but a few of the teachers were on her side, and offered her a great deal of encouragement. June and I started going back to church, and the church members were all glad to have us back. We even had the preacher over and studied God's plan of salvation and studied the Bible once a week with him at home in order to get June baptized and start a new life in Christ. We went pretty regularly. I don't know what happened, but we never finished the home study, and eventually just quit going.

We went over to David Barker's about twice or three times a week, and he used to be our next door neighbor, but married a gal who was a lot older than he was but she had a farm and on it was a horse. They hated the horse because it had kicked David in the back, and he had already had back trouble for years. They said you couldn't catch the horse, and he wasn't to be trusted. June would go for walks in the pasture and the horse would follow her around, and one day the horse came up so close behind her she stopped and reached back without turning around and actually got to pet him. He was only about a year old and June started calling him Thunder. Once, down at the stock pond, June was bending over looking into the water and the horse came up and pushed June in the pond and whinnied and whinnied like he was laughing at her. She crawled out up on the bank and the horse came up to her and she petted it. The horse always came running up to see June as we drove up after that. I ended up trading a .270 caliber deer rifle for that horse, and we found a friend where we could keep it after a lot of looking. We then went and got the horse but thought we were going to break his neck trying to get him in the horse trailer. It took two ropes and four men to get him to load. He kind of got banged up and a cut on his front leg though. Before unloading him, we cut his halter off, because it was a pony halter and it had been on so long that it had grown into his face and was so tight it made sores under it. After that, the horse showed his appreciation for getting him out of the pain of that little halter.

After school every day, we had to tend to the horse and feed him hay. June had already been reading a lot about horses and knew a lot already. We were having a hard time trying to find someone to saddle-break him, but he let June put the saddle on with no problems. June was only 4'10" at the time, but she was strong like a tomboy. One day she said, "Dad, watch out for me, I'm gonna see if he'll let me sit on him," and she did, with no problems. She didn't try to go anywhere just yet, but that was quite an accomplishment not to get bucked of. It wasn't long before she was riding Thunder, and he never did buck once.

I had told June we couldn't have anything to do with Augie anymore, because people would be watching her to see if they got back together. I could tell that didn't go over very well. She had been back with me for only a few weeks when the law came out to arrest me because June had written a confession that I killed Barb and signed my name to it. The Texas Ranger was called, and he said June probably wrote it. I never saw it, but for the night they let June stay down with the neighbors who did hard drugs and stayed drunk a lot. That really got me. I got her back, and while she was in school one day, I found an address on the other side of the lake and I was pretty sure it was a place Augie owned. I confronted June with it, and she said she didn't know where it came from. I said, "I know who will know," so I went to Fitts's Lumber where Lester Butt's wife ran the store, and as I entered the front of the store she started jumping up and down and patting her lips sounding like an Indian around a campfire. I was there to ask her about the address, but she was making such a commotion at the register that I stopped, backed out of the store and said, "You know, if it wasn't for good people like you, I would have a wife right now," and left.

Not long after that, the deputy called and asked me if I was going to be home. I said I had to run to the grocery store, but I would be right back, and he said "No, just stay put. I want to bring you your papers from court," so I waited. He walked in the yard carrying an empty box. That was to get in the house. While he was asking me about the trouble I'd had at Fitts's that day, two more deputies walked in. I told them how she acted, and they didn't believe me, and arrested me for threatening to shoot everyone in the store. I said that was a made-up story, but they gave June back to the dopers and put me in jail. It was on a weekend, so I had to stay until my mom could come bail me out on Monday. The girl who filled out the papers on me worked at the register beside Mrs. Butt, and she was shacked up with Lester Junior, and she was a convicted felon herself. Mrs. Butt signed the papers, but they had to get Judge Leach to order my arrest because if Jake Butt, the JP, signed it, it would have been Butt, Butt and Butt having me arrested. All Augie's friends. When I got out of jail, two of the deputies told me it might be best if I just sold out and left this area. I had so much dealings with the chief of police, and he saw what was happening. He even apologized to me and said, "We are only hourly workers and we have to do what we are told." I often wondered if June had called ahead of me and told Fitts's I was coming to the store, because it was a trap for me.

The day I got out of jail, a long-time old-timer came to visit me, but we talked out by his truck on the county road. He told me that his grandson worked at Fitts's Lumber and that he saw what they did to me. I said "Great, then I can sue them." He said no, that he would lose his job if he did that, and times were hard, so he couldn't help me even knowing what they were doing to me. Now I had to go to the county attorney and talk to him about setting up a court date for a violistic threat, which could mean jail time—the same attorney that did a summary judgment on me for the subdivision. He acted like he was my friend and said "Listen, I can talk to the judge for you and just get you out with a small fine, and this matter will be forgotten." I said, "That sounds better than fighting City Hall—Butt, Butt and Butt." He said, "I'll be right back. Just hang tight." I said "OK." He said, "OK, let's go talk to Judge Leach, but when he asks you how you plead, just tell him 'No contest, Your Honor.'" I said "OK." He came back in and said, "The judge will see you now." Judge Leach told me a violistic threat was a serious matter, and that it could be punishable by some ridiculous amount plus jail time, and asked, "How do you plead?" I forgot what to say, and turned and looked back at Bobby Neil, the county attorney, and he said for me, "No contest, Your Honor." The judge said, "OK, go outside and I'll review this case and call you back in a few minutes." When I came back in, he said, "OK, viewing the severity of the crime, I order you to pay $500.00 today and $60 a month for two years, and you will be on probation and report to your probation officer on the first of every month and pay this in a money order to the County of Saline in person or be put in jail." That was a hard blow, and I was again taken to the cleaners.

I just kept getting deeper all the time. I withdrew from everyone in the subdivision and in town, and started shopping in Many, Louisiana. I stayed out of town after that. I only went to the bank when I had to, because I had direct deposit, and mailed in my bills. I just worked at home and took care of the horse. I even refused to do body and paint work any more or have anything to do with anybody in the subdivision that even knew the Butts. Some of the people who worked for the Butts came to get estimates, and I would tell them, "Sorry, I don't work for anybody having anything to do with the Butts."

June and I had to sit down and talk all of this over, and I told her, "Well, now that I have to pay this money out every month, and if they keep doing these things to me, it looks like we'll have to sell out and move." She sure didn't want that. We talked about her lawyer, and Augie, and she started telling me about all kinds of stuff. She told me that her lawyer wanted her to fly in his personal small airplane, but she said he would get her loaded on beer and want to fly and her to fly with him, but the man at the airport told her he wouldn't if he was her, because he drinks too much, so she never went up with him. She also told me that the lawyer went to Augie's houseboat, and I was really interested in that. That was when June was in detention in Lufkin before her trial. Now I understood why I wasn't allowed in the courtroom—because he was building a case against my wife and I to run us down enough to get everyone to feel sorry for June, being raised by such unworthy parents. If I had been in the courtroom, I would have heard all of his lies about us and make a lot of trouble for the court, and in this way it would be a pushover to get her off. She also said Augie got mad at the lawyer because he would help himself to Augie's freezers and take a lot of frozen catfish fillets when he would come and Augie would not be there. Augie finally ran the lawyer off, June said. The lawyer never once came to my house or visited me. That is why I think her confessions were thrown out and Lester was probably the one to get June's lawyer, but I will never know, I guess.

She also told me that her foster parents would get kids from the courts of her lawyer, and it was a way of making extra money, keeping all these kids, but it was awful having to share clothes and eating at cheap places or fast foods and a lot of soup or one-meal dishes. Now I figured out why she wanted to come back home—because we ate a lot of deep-fried pork and chicken and shrimp breaded. She couldn't do artwork because the other kids would get in it, and they wouldn't buy her any paints or paintbrushes. She really did miss home and the relaxed atmosphere, and she had to take turns doing dishes where she never had to at home. She never hesitated in helping me tape off a car or truck so I could paint it, or help me pulling dents with a winch and pulling on the slide hammer on body work. She never back-talked me, and I never raised my voice, and she liked working with me, it seemed. She always helped me rebuild a carburetor because she had both hands and could get into tiny places with her small hands and enjoyed learning how things worked.

I started getting notes sent home from the teacher saying June wasn't turning in her work and getting zeroes, and it was from only a couple teachers. The other subjects were fine. I had that problem in junior high and knew what she was going through. I would go to school and talk to the teachers and even help June get her lessons, and she still got zeroes on lessons I helped her with. Either June was losing the lessons, or the teachers were. My oldest daughter from a previous marriage had sent me a new computer all the way from Erie, Pennsylvania. Now I had to learn to use it, so I went to the library and checked out a book called Computers for Dummies. It took me three days to read it cover to cover and June had learned the computer in school. I got online one day, and to surprise June, picked her up at noon, checked her out of school and said, "I'm homeschooling you." She was so happy, and really studied hard every day, and graduated two years ahead of her class with a 3.3 average.

On her sixteenth birthday, I bought her a new 2006 Honda Rebel motorcycle on payments, and when she got her diploma for high school, I took her to Natchitoches, Louisiana, and took her to where you can hire a helicopter to fly you over town and we had a ball. Just before I took June out of school, she had made a new girlfriend who seemed to be a real pal and didn't care whether she killed her mother or not like so many did. June had run into her a few times while riding her Honda to Logan's Point, a small settlement where out-of-town fishermen rented cabins to fish. There was a big store and gas station, and when June would stop to get gasoline for her bike, she would see her friend. June asked me if she could spend the night sometime, and so they did. June got me off to the side and said, "She's wearing me out, Dad.

She gets in all my stuff." I told her, "Just find something to do." Well, June got out the paints and let that other girl paint on her own picture, too. This worked pretty well, but that only lasted probably an hour and a half, and after watching a little bit of TV they decided to bed down. I had built June bunk beds. They would be okay there.

We got up the next morning, and since it was Saturday now, they walked down to Carrice Creek about ¾ mile away through the subdivision and played on the playground and walked back. We took that girl home after lunch and then came back home. On the way back, June was complaining, "I didn't know she was like that." She said that before she asked anyone else over, she was going to have to get to know them a little better. Once we got home, June started straightening her things up. She found her whole drawer of underwear missing, and a few other items like keepsake pretties she had were also missing. I walked into the back bedroom, and when I looked out the window I noticed all the little round holes in the curtains and it looked like someone had held a lit cigarette to the mesh curtain and burned round holds. It wasn't until later the next day that she went to get one of her oldie goldie CDs out of the case, and the case was empty. When she started checking other cases, she had been cleaned out of about 100 CDs and they were all oldie goldies by the original artists like Elvis, Neil Diamond, Harry Chapin, the Bee Gees, and no telling how much money she had invested in those CDs because I let her get them one or two at a time when we shopped at Wal-Mart since she was 6 or 7 years old. I had noticed when we took that girl home that she had to make a couple of trips to put her things in the truck to leave, and when we picked her up to come stay the night, she wasn't carrying anything. 2 + 2 again.

Living in a subdivision that was mostly retired people, June was having to bring in someone her own age to be friends with. It was hard to do with everyone knowing about Mom's death and June's trial. I felt sorry for June, but didn't know how to fix that problem. Horses and a motorcycle took the place of friends, I guess. Now that I look back on it, I realize June was using her girlfriend as a scapegoat to cover up the real truth, which was that that was June's way of inventing a way to get some more of her things out of the house and start moving her personal prized possessions to Augie's house without me suspecting anything—and it worked.

An old friend of mine I had met shortly after moving to the subdivision, Paul Hensickle, came over one day needing help with his old Chevy van because the gears were going out on the adjustable steering wheel, and I told him how to and where to go to get another steering column cheap, and he told me all of the problems he had been having going through a divorce and all, and I had plenty to tell him, all right. Then I didn't see him for about a year after that, and he came around again, and this time he was driving an older Cadillac, but it was like new. Well, he invited June and me over to play Texas Hold 'Em and I didn't see any harm in that, as we had been friends for years and he was about 68 years old. I knew he smoked pot, but that wasn't a big deal, and he used to be a heavy beer drinker. I used to work for him occasionally, as he was a brick layer, and he used to come get me and I would run the concrete mixer and keep mud on his board up on the scaffold. This was back when Barb and I were first married, and June was too young to remember. He had gotten a DWI since I had last seen him and had gone to rehab and all, and was pretty well straightened out. He was a guide for bass fishing and had a nice boat with a big new motor on it. He told me that while his license was pulled from the DWI, he had borrowed a friend's car to go to Wal-Mart in Many, Louisiana. When he parked the car in Wal-Mart's parking lot, a church bus pulled up behind him. He was standing at the back of the car replacing stop-light bulbs with the trunk open, and the bus backed into him, pinning him against his car. He was hollering and shouting in pain as his legs got pinned between the bumpers. He couldn't walk for a while, and he sued the church people and won. That's why he had the Cadillac, and he was waiting for the rest of the money from the lawsuit to buy him a house. He bought a nice place, but it was in the subdivision. It was a nice house, with a garage and all. June and I started going over there a lot and playing cards and going fishing with him and even put a floor on his pontoon boat, carpeted it and took his outboard motor off and put a truck motor inboard in it.

I didn't worry about Paul, because he was too old, and he also had heart trouble. We had a lot of fun and spent a lot of time over at his house, till all the rumors of June and Paul being together too much. Paul also bought a Ford truck that was almost new. We went to Jasper one day to drop off a prop for his bass boat, and the Honda motorcycle dealer was next door, so June and I went in and she got to sit on a brand new Honda Rebel 250 cc motorcycle and fell in love with it, and June was about to be 16 years old. June had been studying for her drivers' license, and I had been letting her drive on the back roads going to feed the horse. On her 16th birthday, we went down in Paul's new truck and bough that same bike, and she was a happy camper now. She kept it clean and rode it with pride.

June got to go places with Paul, just those two, and I was glad I didn't have to worry about her. A lot of people were talking, but I didn't care. Paul had a heart attack and ended up in Lufkin hospital, and we went and brought him home as he had to have a bypass. After his bypass, he was a changed man. Now he was sarcastic and did things that pissed people off at him and he started coming on to June just like Augie had. He would be driving along and get stuck on purpose so I would have to hitchhike to get our truck and chain to pull his out, I guess so he could be alone with my daughter. We were shooting bottle rockets off of the houseboat, and he wanted me to go up to the bank and shoot bottle rockets at the egrets because we had a spotlight on the trees and the birds would fly out of the trees by the hundreds and circle in the dark. It was funny, but after we came home, June told me Paul had grabbed her and kissed her and got his saliva in her mouth and it was nasty and had a tobacco smell. I asked her why she didn't tell me then, and she said she was afraid of what I might do to him. Well, there went our friendship.

Being a single parent was really trying most of the time, and I was trying to make the best of it. We withdrew again from everyone and just did motorcycles and horses. I traded for me a Honda Rebel 250 cc and rigged it up with a foot clutch on the right side so I could ride with June. I really enjoyed riding a motorcycle again, and loved to ride and even go through the turns on the dirt country road with the back tire trying to wash out on me and ever went down. June had her drivers' license now, and got to go over to a girlfriend from high school days and visit and draw horses for that girl's mom and dad. June traded horses and got a huge quarter horse, and it was older than the papers said. It wanted to run all the time and you couldn't stop him. He didn't have any brakes. We even used a bit with a lot of leverage and it made the horse's mouth bloody but she had to trade him off and got a mare and a colt. Shortly after getting this one, the mare kicked June and broke her arm, and she had to wear a cast for six weeks, but soon got over it. She spent lots of time on horseback down all the county roads, and one time she and a girl she knew in school were riding back to where we now kept the horses over at Piney Point, about a five-mile ride. It was late in the day in October, and the girl knew a shortcut through the woods. Well, it got dark, and being overcast, it got dark early, and I had to call the law and report June couldn't be found. We didn't know they had tried a shortcut, and she had never gotten off the county roads before now. The deputies and game wardens searched for a couple hours and sent for bloodhounds 150 miles away. We were told to quit looking, that they would handle it since it was now after midnight. They were not dressed for the cold because it was about 80 degrees when they left and now it was only 50 degrees and neither one had a jacket. It was another tense moment—two girls on horseback disappearing. They found them at 2 AM, deep in the woods. It only took the bloodhounds minutes to trail them in pitch black darkness. That was a relief. The girls were hugging the horses for warmth and just waiting to be found. After they loaded up the horses, the game warden explained why he didn't want anyone in the woods. The fish and game department had released a couple thousand rattlesnakes in Saline County to re-introduce them back in the wild to control rodents. It was nice the subdivision was leaving us alone. It was all about fun on horseback and motorcycles.

June started looking for a job, and I traded Mom's '66 Ford for a nice-looking 1998 Dodge truck. It was black and chrome and a V-6 short wheel base. She loved it at first, but it was a full size truck and set up real high and she couldn't reach the pedals, so I made steel blocks and raised the seat up. After feeding the horse one evening, she didn't get home till 11 PM and I was about to go looking for her when she drove up. She came in and said, "Dad, I kinda had a little accident." I said, "What happened?" and she said, "Well, I put the truck in park running and got out, and it backed into the woods with the driver's door opened and a tree caught the door and stopped the truck." I said, "OK, now let's go out and look." She had to drive home with the door open because it had been bent backwards. I said, "OK, let's fix it." I put a chain on the door and put the truck in park and used a chain hoist to pull the door back into place where we could at least close the door for the night. We got through shortly after midnight.

She couldn't find work, and thought she might try college. We went all over taking entrance exams for the next few months, but just missed passing grades. She heard of a junior college in Many that might accept her, and they did, and she chose nurse's aide. So now my daughter who had been through all these hard times is now a college student. Life has so many ups and downs, I thought. I had got stuck taking care of the horse, and she had sold the mare, and I had bought her a lot of new tack and saddles. I didn't mind my troubled daughter was now in college. She made good grades and everything went smooth in her seventeenth year. We ate out at different restaurants about twice a week, sometimes three times. She still hadn't dated anyone or wanted to. After passing her first semester, it was getting close to Christmas, and I had ordered her some real Elvis Presley jewelry that used to be owned by Elvis fans back in the 60's, and she loved them.

I had a VA appointment on December 23, 2006, and her birthday was December 21. I told her, "I don't know what I'm going to do, but at 18 you are officially a legal grownup. I'll always be here for you, but just stay out of trouble. Everyone will be watching to see if you go to Augie, and that could be trouble for you, so beware of that and just don't burn any bridges." She got in a hurry to sell her horse and I couldn't imagine that. Then, on December 22, she asked me what time I was leaving to go to Lufkin where my appointment was, and I said "Early, because it's an hour's drive and I have to be there at 8 AM." She said, "Can I go with you, because now I don't have a horse? Can I get some kind of a pet at the pet store?" I said "Sure, but you gotta get up on time." She said, "What time are you gonna be back?" and I said "Oh, probably about 11:00."

When I got up in the morning, I said, "You better get ready, it's time," and she said, "Dad, I think I'm getting a sore throat, so I better stay home." I said, "OK, see you soon." She said, "OK, Dad." When I got back from Lufkin, I noticed her bike was not in the garage, and there was a note on the table that read, "My friends came over and got me and the bike. Don't worry about me, I'm OK. June."

Now I had told June I was going to go to Gatesville, Texas, for New Year's 2008. I looked in her chest of drawers and she had filled all her drawers with clothes that were old and too small for her and her trophies and all her personal items were gone. One drawer was even full of my socks. I just shook my head in disgust and couldn't believe I had spent the last five years worrying about her and getting her everything she wanted to try and make up for all the hard times thinking maybe she would learn to love me as a good parent and still be in contact with me, as she was all I had left. I went over to Mr. David Rivers and talked to him and really got filled in on the last two years.

You see, David was a retired widower, and he had been 68 years old now for several years. About three years ago, a fellow I did a lot of repair work for on his company trucks let us move the horse over to his property by David's, and David loved animals of all kinds, so he of course liked June's horse and began helping her and I a lot building fence and watering the horse and hauling round bales which weigh from 500 to 1000 pounds and never charged us for a thing. Now David told me that June didn't like David coming over all the time she was with the horse because she had a cell phone and would be on it all the time. He didn't know who she would talk to for long periods of time, but she would hide it when David would come over to the horse. I had bought June a cell phone, but she left it at the house and wouldn't carry it with her. She said it wouldn't get reception anywhere. I had told her when I gave it to her that the phone company keeps records, and if they were ever checked it would show if she called Augie or not. June was telling me that David would always want her to do things his way with the horse and he didn't know anything about horses. She didn't want David helping her. Now David tells me the reason he let up on watering the horse and helping her like he did was that June had told an older lady down the street that David was making advances on her, and that lady went to David and tried to shame him for messing with that little girl. It scared David so bad he even went to an attorney and talked to him about it, and was advised just to stay away from her. I asked him why didn't he tell me about this, and he said he liked me as a friend and didn't want to cause any trouble between us. Now June was 18 years old and she was gone.

I had planned to be in Gatesville for New Year's, so I just took some extra clothes and set out to find some of my old friends and get away from all this shit. As far as I was concerned, I did my best, and I got her through high school and into college. She had a nice truck that was paid for, a brand new motorcycle paid for, and she was gone. It really hurt one more time really bad that she had to do me that way, leaving the way she did. I went to Gatesville and stayed at a motel and went out on New Year's. I didn't meet anyone I knew at the club, but I did make a new friend that knew me because his best friend was my best friend and he had died of cancer the year before. The town gunsmith had talked to this guy so much about me. He figured I was the one armed bandit. You see, I used to shoot a lot of pool in the old days, and I only had one arm. So when he saw me shooting pool, he figured I was Keith's friend Bob Thomson. Another friend, Bobby Sheets, met me and we got in his 1936 Mack truck on New Year's Day and he hauled me all over town and took me to see a lot of my old friends which was a lot of fun.

I then headed back to Hilltown, Texas, and it was 250 miles. All the way home I was wondering where June was and why she had done me this way again. Most fathers wouldn't have taken her back, they tell me. Anyway, when I got back home, I had a message on my recorder in a man's voice and he said he wanted to let me know that in case I didn't know where June was that she was with Augie and the place she will be in for the holidays is down in Beaumont, Texas, and gave me the phone number. I had Mom call the number in case they had caller ID, and it was Augie's mother's house. Mom asked for June, and they hung up.

I figured, well, it's just me, I guess, in this big old house. June left her truck but it was still in my name. Now that June was gone, I had time to go through the house and go through all of the drawers and pictures and papers and clothes. All the closets were so full, the floors were piled knee deep. The clothes hangers on the rods were so close with clothes on them, and all the dressers and chests of drawers were so packed it was hard to get the drawers open and closed. I had at least 30 rods and reels that were in good working order. One closet was upstairs and at least 18 feet in length, and I started there first. I had built a gun cabinet in the floor of the closet so I could put my guns where they would have to use a phillips head screwdriver to take the closet apart to find them if anyone ever broke in to steal anything. It took me about four hours just to get from one end to the other because I was bagging up the clothes to give them to the needy. When I got to the other end, I could work on the floor of the closet. Now I came to a lot of folded blankets and sheets and boxes of stuff too good to throw away, but I had no need for the stuff. It was things my wife and June had put up that were out of the way in the closet. I came upon an old steel circuit breaker box I had made for June just after Barb was cremated. I built it for June to keep her jewelry and silver change, money and such and put a hasp on it for a lock. It had a lock on it, and I had no idea where the keys were. I shook it, and it sounded like papers in it, so I thought I had better open it in case it was hidden cash. I pried on it with a big screwdriver, and it was too strong, so I went out to the garage and got a big crowbar and held one end with my foot and pried on it with the other. It was hard and took a few struggling minutes, but I was finally able to break the weld at the seams. Inside, I found one more confession June wrote for me, admitting shooting Mom, and my signature written by June. That was so disheartening I had to just sit down and rethink what this meant. I got to thinking. June figured I wouldn't find this for a long time—or there were plans something was going to happen to me too—what now—what? This would be found and there would be no one to say it wasn't my handwriting—what?

At first this made me so mad I had to have time to think what to do, but it sure wasn't hard to find the time. With no one around and no work, all I had was time and all the heartache. I had a hard time sleeping with all these thoughts trying to figure out what I was going to do now. I called my mom at the rest home and now she was almost 90 years old and told her about the box and June writing a confession for me, and Mom said, "Well, don't that beat all." She said, "I wish I could talk to June. I would like to set her straight or at least find out something," and I said, "I don't know how much good it will do you, but I have Augie's telephone number down on the pontoon boat." Mom called there and asked for June. She thought it was Augie that answered. It was a man, and he said "Who is this?" and "June is not here, but I can have her call you."

Mom called me back and was kind of shook up, but she said, "I guess that's it for June." The next day, June visited her grandmother at the rest home in St. Angustine, Texas, and they had a little talk. June said she was fine but was living in Shreveport working for Exxon, a big oil refinery, and was making lots of money. Mom asked her, "There is something I have to know and I want the truth. Did you shoot your mom?" June said yes, and gave no explanation, but got quiet, and that pretty well ended the conversation. June left un-emotionally. Then my mom called me and told me about June coming to see her and said she seemed happy and was dressed in blue jeans like she always was and didn't stay very long but just wanted to come over and see her in person. That was the last time my mom ever got to see June.

I guess I'll have to accept it and I don't want anything to do with that little girl anymore. I just can't understand how anyone could do that to their own mother. I told Mom it's hard to believe how she could be so quiet and not give us any trouble in any other way, and do this. I guess it was the day after that that I started burning everything. All the bagged-up clothes, and most of June's and Mom's keepsakes, and everything out of the drawers and chests except just the clothes I needed. I called up my black friends that had the horses and told them I would sell them all of June's tack and three saddles, and two of them were practically new. They came over and paid me in cash, and the three to four-hundred-dollar saddles sold for $150 for both of them and $25 for the older one. I told them June had went to Augie and she was gone. June had spent many hours riding on the county roads with them on trail rides.

I then started eating out a lot for supper by myself in places where the waiters used to see June and me together. At night I started going to Many, Louisiana, and shooting pool a lot because before I met my Barb that's what I used to do. I surprised a lot of people as I would win a lot, but I wanted to get back to the way I used to play. I bought a pool table and put it in the dining room and just played pool, day and night, for a couple months. Father's Day came around and the phone didn't ring one time and nobody stopped by as I shot pool all day long. I had been trying to sell June's Dodge truck as it just sat there and I finally sold it to the neighbor. He said, "Are you going to sell the house too?" and I said, "Might as well." I told him $12,000 for garage tools, silverware, everything but my bed and just a few tools. The next day I said, "How much have you got?" and he said, "$8,000." I said "OK." I moved back to Gatesville, my old hometown.

As I look back, I will always love my daughter—just because she is my daughter, I guess, and for the fact that if we would not have lived where we did and in such a troubled area with people that had so much influence on turning her against her parents, everything would be a whole different ballgame.

www.ingramcontent.com/pod-product-compliance
Ingram Content Group UK Ltd.
Pitfield, Milton Keynes, MK11 3LW, UK
UKHW041917190726
13854UKWH00003B/1294